CASTAWAYS
IN LILLIPUT

CASTAWAYS
in LILLIPUT

Henry Winterfeld

Illustrated by William M. Hutchinson
Translated by Kyrill Schabert

AN ODYSSEY/HARCOURT YOUNG CLASSIC
HARCOURT, INC.
San Diego   New York   London

www.HarcourtBooks.com

First Harcourt Young Classics edition 2002
First Odyssey Classics edition 1990
First published in the United States in 1960

Library of Congress Cataloging-in-Publication Data
Winterfeld, Henry.
[Telegramm aus Liliput. English]
Castaways in Lilliput/Henry Winterfeld; illustrated by William M. Hutchinson;
translated from the German by Kyrill Schabert.
p. cm.
Originally published: San Diego: Harcourt Brace Jovanovich, 1958.
"An Odyssey/Harcourt Young Classic."
Summary: Three Australian children, adrift on a rubber raft, are cast ashore in a
strange land of tiny people.
[1. Fantasy.] I. Hutchinson, William M., ill. II. Schabert, Kyrill. III. Title.
PZ7.W766Cas 2002
[Fic]—dc21 2002024381
ISBN 0-15-216298-4 ISBN 0-15-216286-0 (pb)

Printed in the United States of America

A C E G H F D B
A C E G H F D B (pb)

To Marianne and Thomas

Contents

CASTAWAYS
IN LILLIPUT

1

Worse and Worse

"Now we are in a nice fix!" cried Ralph. "We can't buck the wind any longer."

Frantically, Peggy and Jim looked toward the shore. The beach by now was only a thin white line, and the bald mountains on the horizon looked no bigger than hills. They shimmered distantly through the haze of a subtropical noonday. Of the low ranch house and the barns, which stood among the eucalyptus trees, only the red roofs remained visible.

"Can we make it back?" Peggy asked anxiously.

"Not like this," said Ralph, and wiped the sweat off his forehead. Even on the water the heat was insufferable, in spite of the strong wind.

"But that's terrible," cried Peggy. "I want to listen to 'Romeo and Juliet' on the radio tonight. Mary Higgins, from London, is playing Juliet, and Billy Walton, Romeo."

Jim turned toward her. " 'Romeo and Juliet,' "

he scoffed. "You'll be lucky if you're still alive by tonight."

"Don't scare her," Ralph shouted angrily. "Why don't you try to paddle harder instead?"

"I'm paddling like mad," cried Jim, "but it's no use. We're drifting further out all the time."

Before long the water was whipped into white-caps, and the small rubber raft bounced up and down like a ball. Now and then cool, salty spray would pour over the children, soaking them to the skin. All they had on were shorts and shirts because they had played tennis in the morning. Later they had gone down to the beach in search of adventure. Jim had taken along his toy gun and Peggy a small canvas bag with a shoulder strap. They had eaten their sandwiches some time ago, and Peggy had only a few odds and ends left in the bag. It was lucky that Ralph and Jim had on their tropical helmets because the sun was directly over them, scorching them like a flamethrower. Peggy wore a pretty white cap with a plastic green visor. Now it was completely soaked.

Ralph sat in the back, on the rim of the rubber raft. Jim was kneeling up front, and between them crouched Peggy, on the wet bottom, which was nothing but a thin sheet of rubber. Each time a wave thumped against the bottom of the raft, it was as though someone slapped Peggy, with the accompanying sound of exploding firecrackers. Peggy kept up her courage and didn't budge for fear that it might interfere with the boys' paddling.

"I'm tired!" exclaimed Jim suddenly, and threw his paddle into the raft. He was puffing like a locomotive and trying to rub the salt water out of his eyes.

"Oh, don't act like that!" scolded Peggy. "Let me paddle." She wanted to crawl forward, but Ralph yelled, "Stay put, Peggy; the raft might capsize!"

Frightened, Peggy slumped back. By now, Ralph too had stopped paddling. He slid to the bottom of the raft in a state of exhaustion.

"The wind is offshore and freshening." He groaned. "All we can do is wait until it dies down or changes direction."

"We'll be dead by then!" cried Jim in desperation.

"Fiddlesticks!" said Ralph. "The wind often changes."

He was scared himself but did not want to admit it, since he was older than the others and felt responsible for them. Peggy and Jim were sister and brother. Peggy was eleven years old, Jim nine. Their father was one of the wealthiest sheep breeders on the west coast of Australia. Ralph was the son of the ranch superintendent.

"If only we hadn't found this silly raft," muttered Peggy.

"Nobody asked you to come along," snapped Jim.

"You have a nerve," said Peggy. "As though you hadn't talked me into it."

"How could we guess that a wind would come up so suddenly?" replied Jim, trying to defend himself.

Ralph, with a guilty conscience, remained silent. The children had found the rubber raft by accident on the beach under a mangrove bush. Two paddles were in it, and Jim, in high spirits, suggested paddling out to sea for a bit. Ralph saw no objection. At first, Peggy had not wanted to come along, but she finally gave in because she did not want to stay behind on the deserted beach. The sea was as smooth as glass, there was not a breath of air, and they had paddled farther out than they had meant to. Suddenly, a wind had sprung up and they found themselves drifting farther and farther away from shore into the open ocean.

"The waves are getting worse and worse," Peggy

complained, "and all that spray pouring into the boat!"

By now, the children were sitting in water almost up to their waists. Ralph looked around.

"We have to bail," he said.

"But there isn't anything to bail with," said Jim.

"Our helmets!" cried Ralph hopefully. "We can use them for buckets."

Feverishly, Ralph and Jim scooped the water over the side with their helmets, but it was a long time before most of the water was bailed. Then they lay down, tired out. Doggedly, Peggy continued bailing.

"I've done it," she called after a while, catching her breath. "It's almost dry."

"Don't stop!" yelled Jim, without moving.

"Why don't you bail yourself, you lazybones?" said Peggy indignantly. "I'm pooped too." She tore her sopping wet cap from her head, wrung it, and furiously slapped it back on her dripping hair.

"Take a rest," said Ralph. "We'll bail some more later." He waited until the raft rose on another wave to look toward the shore.

"You can't see land anymore," he muttered in dismay.

"Oh, dear," called Peggy. "What will our parents think if we don't get home in time? Mommy had asked the seamstress, Miss Smith, to come this afternoon. I was to get a new dress for school opening. She'll be there at three o'clock."

"It must be later than that," said Ralph, nervously squinting at the sun.

Peggy looked at him in panic. Suddenly, Jim jumped up.

"Perhaps they'll be looking for us with planes," he said excitedly. He threw down his gun and hastily tore off his shirt and waved it like fury. At that moment, the raft was hit by a good-sized wave, and

he fell overboard, head first. He went under but almost immediately came up croaking, "Help! Help!" With one hand, he held on to his shirt, using the other to swim after the raft. The waves kept going over his head, and he would soon have gone under for good if Ralph had not leaned far out and grabbed him by the hair in the nick of time.

"Quick! Quick, Peggy!" he yelled. "Shift your weight to the other side or we'll capsize."

Peggy flung herself to the other side and leaned out over the water, while Ralph helped Jim climb back onto the raft.

"Gee whiz!" sputtered Jim, spitting out a lot of water. "I was sure I was going to drown."

"You could never have caught up with the raft," said Ralph. "We're drifting much too fast."

"It was the shirt that bothered me," said Jim angrily.

"Put it on," said Ralph. "Otherwise you'll get a sunburn. And don't try this kind of acrobatics again. You were lucky that I caught hold of you."

"But we must signal," replied Jim a bit meekly, "or else the planes won't see us."

"We can do that sitting down," said Ralph.

But there was no plane to be seen, least of all to be heard. The wind was howling and the waves were pounding. For some time a flock of albatross had been circling above the raft. They never stopped shrieking, and they eyed the children with curiosity. Forlorn, the children were thinking of their homes, wishing that they had never found the rubber raft.

"Our parents will be terribly upset," said Peggy with a deep sigh.

"Unfortunately, they won't know that we found the raft," said Ralph, anxiously looking at her out of the corner of his eye. "They'll look everywhere except on the water."

"And they had forbidden us to go rowing," said Peggy reproachfully. "They wouldn't even let us swim in the ocean because of the sharks."

"Boy!" exclaimed Jim. He looked at the sea and shuddered. He had not thought of sharks when he was swimming after the raft.

"Perhaps a ship will see us," said Peggy.

"There're never any ships around here," said Ralph ominously. "The wind is out of the east, and we're drifting toward the west. That's way outside all the ship lanes."

"But that's awful!" exclaimed Peggy. "How long will we drift this way?"

"Perhaps we'll land on an island," said Jim, looking at Ralph expectantly.

"There are no islands around," said Ralph. He was fond of reading books about explorers, and geography was his best subject in school.

"But there are islands everywhere," ventured Peggy meekly.

"Not around here," said Ralph. "I think the next island between us and Africa is Mauritius."

"Mauritius?" asked Jim. "How far is that?"

"About four thousand miles," said Ralph.

9

"Four . . . four thousand miles?" stammered Peggy. "And nothing in between?"

"No," said Ralph, "only sky and water."

Peggy and Jim were horrified.

"You're a liar!" roared Jim in a rage. Then he threw himself flat on his stomach and howled louder than the wind.

2

Some Savages Do Speak English

Something hard bumped against the raft. The children woke up frightened. It was pitch dark. They must have fallen asleep.

"What happened?" groaned Ralph, and touched his aching head.

They had been shaken by the bump, but now the raft lay motionless.

"Where are we?" murmured Peggy, gasping for air. Jim had fallen on top of her, and she couldn't budge. "Get off me!" she yelled. "You're squashing me."

"But I can't see anything!" Jim murmured sleepily, aimlessly thrashing his hands and feet in the water still inside the raft.

Ralph bent over the side and yelled in glee, "Hurray! We've hit a beach! Come on! We're safe!"

He leaped out like lightning. Head first, Jim

tumbled after him. Peggy too wanted to get out, but she couldn't stand up.

"Help, my legs," she pleaded. "They're dead."

Ralph shook with laughter. He was so happy over the sudden rescue that he could have danced a jig.

"They've fallen asleep," he called. "Mine feel like jelly. That's because we have been so cramped."

He pulled Peggy out of the raft and dropped her on the wet sand. Jim skipped around like a dervish and yelled without stopping, "Land! Land! Land!"

Then he threw himself down and gratefully kissed the sand. He once had read a book about some shipwrecked people who had kissed the beach when they had finally reached land. But he jumped up quickly and loudly blew his nose because he had stuck it too far into the sand. Eagerly, Ralph looked around. There was no moon, and only a few stars flickered through the haze. All he could see was the glimmer of the beach nearby. He could hear the pounding of the surf. Once in a while the outrunner of a breaker would lick the children's feet. Then the water would recede with a soft hiss. The wind was still blowing from the ocean but no longer as hard.

"A high wave must have thrown us onto the beach," said Ralph.

"Have we landed on an island?" asked Jim, still desperately blowing his nose.

"There are no islands around here," said Ralph stubbornly.

"Well, we've got to be somewhere," cried Peggy. She was sitting on the beach busily massaging her legs. She had taken off her cap, and her wet hair had blown into her face.

"Perhaps we're back home again," Jim suggested hopefully. "While we were asleep, the wind changed and blew us back home! I'll go and see where we've landed."

"Stay where you are," ordered Ralph. "First, we have to secure the rubber raft."

"Why?" asked Jim impatiently.

"The tide might be low now," said Ralph. "At high tide the raft will be swept away."

"Let it . . ." called Peggy. "I hate the thing. I shall never get into a rubber raft again." The mere thought of it made her feel sick.

"The raft doesn't belong to us," said Ralph firmly. He took it by the rope that hung around the side in loops and tried to pull it up the beach. But it was too heavy.

"Give me a hand," he called. "It's full of water."

Cautiously, Peggy got up and examined her legs. Then she helped Ralph and Jim to tip the raft. After they had spilled out the water, Jim picked up his gun and hung it over his shoulder while Ralph put the tropical helmets and the paddles back into the raft. Then he looked about searchingly. The beach was not very wide. It rose steeply to a growth of shrubs or something that, in the darkness, looked like shrubs.

"There are bushes up there," said Ralph. "We can lash the raft to them."

Ralph and Jim pulled the raft up the slope and Peggy pushed from behind. After they had reached the top, they blinked in astonishment. The shrubs were not shrubs at all but a sprawling forest of leafy trees. They were old trees with fairly thick trunks but, surprisingly enough, not much taller than the children themselves.

"We aren't home," said Ralph, puzzled.

"Why not?" called Peggy and Jim in disappointment.

"We don't have funny trees like these at home."

"We landed on an island after all," Jim blurted out.

"It must be a crazy island, with trees like these," said Ralph, scratching his head.

"They're oak trees," cried Peggy firmly. "Once Aunt Cornelia, in Sydney, took me to the Botanical

Gardens, where there was the same kind of trees."

"How did you know they were oaks?" asked Jim suspiciously.

"It said so on them," said Peggy.

"Oak trees are at least ten times as tall as we are," said Ralph. "I learned that in our nature class."

"Then they must be dwarf oaks," insisted Peggy, "but oaks they are."

"Perhaps we have landed in a botanical garden," suggested Jim.

"Rubbish!" snapped Ralph. He tried to take a few steps into the forest, but the branches and twigs barred the way.

"Impossible to get through here," he said. "I think we had better leave the raft on the edge of the forest and trust that the tide won't reach that high."

"Let's walk along the beach," proposed Jim. "Perhaps we'll find a bungalow and can ask someone for help."

"Oh, yes!" called Peggy. "I'm dying of hunger and thirst. My stomach is growling. It never does that at home."

"Mine growls too," said Ralph, "but we had better stay here."

"Are you afraid to come along?" asked Peggy, startled.

"Hush! Don't make so much noise," whispered Ralph, and looked around nervously.

"Why not?" asked Peggy uneasily.

"How do we know where we are? There might be savages," he hinted darkly. He sat down by the boat as though wanting to protect it.

"Savages?" breathed Peggy, and quickly moved close to him. With eyes wide open, she stared into the darkness.

"Savages? What kind of savages?" asked Jim.

"Hostile savages," whispered Ralph. "There are headhunters on New Guinea. They ambush people at night and cut their heads off."

"Oh, that shouldn't be allowed!" cried Peggy with a shudder, reaching for her throat.

"But New Guinea is far away from here," said Jim, trembling slightly with fear.

"They say there are headhunters on the other islands," said Ralph.

Jim had lost all desire to go exploring. "Hadn't we better leave?" he asked.

"The island may be uninhabited," said Ralph. "We'll stay here till dawn, but we'll have to be absolutely silent and stay on the lookout. The moment we hear something suspicious, we'll paddle out to sea."

Peggy groaned. Jim sat up and hugged his gun as if it might protect him. Ralph kept his ears cocked. But only the leaves on the strange, small trees rustled in the wind, and from the beach below came the muted rumble of the breakers.

"Oh, if only I were home and in my bed!" murmured Peggy. She could never keep silent for long.

"You two go to sleep," said Ralph. "I'll stand watch."

"But I can't sleep," complained Peggy. "I'm still soaked to the skin and I'm covered with sticky sand. Besides, I have a terrible sunburn on my arms and legs. Mother has a wonderful ointment."

"Quiet! I think I hear something," Ralph interrupted her brusquely.

From somewhere on the beach came the sound of hushed voices. It sounded as though people were excitedly carrying on a whispered conversation.

The children held their breath. The murmur of the voices faded away.

"Those were human beings," said Peggy after a while. "They were speaking English, but I couldn't understand a word."

Ralph nodded in agreement. "They were speaking English all right. They must have been quite far away."

"The people were very near," said Peggy. "I have good ears. My singing teacher, Miss Bock, always tells me so."

"They surely couldn't have been savages," said Jim. "Savages don't speak English."

"Some savages do speak English," Ralph replied.

"People who want to cut off your head don't speak English," insisted Jim angrily. The thought of the headhunters kept bothering him.

"Shall I shout so that they can hear us?" asked Peggy. "I can shout very loud."

"No," said Ralph and stood up. "Stay here and don't move. I'll scout around to see what that could have been." Noiselessly he slipped into the darkness.

Staring into the night, Peggy and Jim felt abandoned. It seemed like ages until Ralph returned. He appeared as suddenly as he had vanished.

"I couldn't discover anything," he reported. He sat down in the sand and said, "Listen. If those were humans, we should find their footprints tomorrow morning. Then we will see whether they wore shoes or not. As a rule, savages don't wear shoes."

He stopped abruptly. A narrow, dazzling streak of light had appeared on the dark sky. It dipped and methodically swept along the edge of the forest. It came closer and closer until it spotted them and caught them in its beam. The children had to close their eyes so as not to be blinded. The light went out, and they gazed into the darkness in complete bewilderment. The night seemed blacker than ever.

"That was a lighthouse," said Jim.

"That was no lighthouse," objected Ralph. "The beam of a lighthouse blinks all night long. Besides, it was much too thin to be the beam of a lighthouse. It was a searchlight."

"You always know better," Jim said indignantly. "It was too a lighthouse! The beam came from far away."

"It came from the sea," said Peggy. "Perhaps it was a ship."

"It didn't come from the sea," said Ralph, "but from somewhere back on the beach."

"Perhaps it was the people whom we heard a little while ago," said Peggy.

"They must have seen us," said Ralph. "Probably they'll come here now."

Tensely, the children waited, but nobody came.

"Maybe they're afraid of us," said Peggy.

"They're pirates!" suggested Jim meekly.

"Pirates don't exist anymore," Ralph retorted.

"Pirates exist everywhere," objected Jim hotly. "I've read that."

"Sure, in your junky books," jeered Ralph.

"You read them yourself, all the time," cried Jim furiously. He was about to say something more but a piercing wail silenced him.

3

The Place Is Bewitched

For at least five minutes the wail continued with a rising and falling pitch. Suddenly it stopped, only to start again farther off. Within a short time the sound seemed to spread over the whole island.

Jim jumped up in panic. "Those are the head-hunters!" he yelled. "Quick, quick, let's escape." Terrified, he yanked at the rubber raft, determined to pull it down to the sea. Ralph grabbed the other end and held onto it.

"Calm down, Jim," he said. "Those aren't savages; they're sirens."

"Let go! Let go!" Jim begged.

"Don't be a fool!" roared Ralph. "I'm telling you those are sirens, just like an air-raid alarm."

"Air raid?" asked Jim, rattled.

"Sure," said Ralph. "Don't you know that we have the same kind of siren on the roof of our fire-house? Listen."

The wail of the siren had changed to a deep grumble. Finally it stopped.

"You see," said Ralph. "Only sirens grumble at the end."

"Perhaps savages grumble at the end, too," said Jim reluctantly.

Ralph paid no more attention to him. He got up and looked around.

"Only civilized people have sirens," he said. "We don't have to be afraid any more. Now I'm really curious about where we are."

It was beginning to get lighter, and it would not be long before the sun would rise. In the east, a few small, pink clouds hovered above the sea. The wind had calmed down and the surf was now only a gentle roll breaking over a distant sandbank. The beach had grown much wider; the tide was probably low. As far as the children could see, the forest with the odd small trees stretched along the coast and extended far inland, over a range of hills that screened off the horizon. A few birds chirped softly; otherwise, there was complete silence. There was neither a house, nor a ship, nor a living soul.

"It's lonely here," said Peggy, dispirited. She looked tired and her hair was hopelessly tangled. The children were weary, hungry, and thirsty. The warm wind during the night had dried their shirts and trousers, leaving them as stiff as washboards.

"My clothes have turned into sandpaper," said Peggy disgustedly. "Everything scratches when I move."

"That's the salt water," said Ralph. "When it evaporates, the salt remains. We'll rinse them out when we find a brook."

"Which way do we walk?" asked Jim, and looked up and down the beach helplessly.

"This way," said Ralph, pointing north. "The beam of the searchlight came somewhere from that direction. We'll look for the footprints. Once we have found them, we'll follow them."

"Oh, what fun! Just like Boy Scouts!" cried Peggy, filled with new enthusiasm. She ran down toward the sea, where her cap was still lying in the sand. She shook it out and put it on. Then she brushed her hair from her face and felt ready for anything.

"Put on your helmet, Jim," said Ralph. "It might get hot again." Full of new vigor, he put on his own and whistled merrily. He was convinced that soon they would find people and help.

"Now, be sharp!" he explained. "We'll spread out and walk up the beach so that we don't miss the tracks."

After just a few paces, Peggy called excitedly, "Here are some!"

Ralph and Jim hurried over. In the damp sand there were tiny footprints, as though a few toy soldiers had marched up to this point and then turned back.

"Those were no human beings," said Ralph, disappointed.

"But they wore shoes," insisted Peggy. She kneeled down to study the tracks more closely. "You can clearly see the soles and heels."

"There are no shoes as small as that."

"Sure there are," said Peggy. "Very small dolls have shoes like that."

"Dolls don't run on the beach at night."

"They were sea gulls," called Jim.

"Sea gulls don't wear shoes, you idiot," said Ralph heatedly.

He was annoyed that they had not found human tracks.

"Perhaps there is some kind of animal with paws that look like shoes," suggested Peggy timidly.

"Some kind of animal doesn't give us anything to eat," growled Ralph. "Let's go! We'll walk on until we find a house or a street."

With his long legs, he strode rapidly ahead,

while Peggy and Jim struggled to keep up with him. Abruptly, Ralph stopped and called, "Here's a rubber raft!"

"Where?" called Peggy and Jim in amazement. They could not see a raft and thought Ralph had lost his mind.

"Right here," Ralph called to them, "in this puddle."

A tiny rubber raft floated in a little pool, still half full of water from the ebbing tide. The raft was no larger than a soup plate but looked just like a real one. There were paddles in it. The rim was inflated and had a string looped around it. The small tracks that the children discovered a short while ago led to the pool and from there to the edge of the forest.

"These animals came by boat," called Peggy.

"Nonsense," said Ralph. "Probably they were curious about it. Animals are always curious."

"The boat is wonderful," Jim called enthusiastically. "I'll take it home with me."

"Are you crazy?" Ralph lit into him. "It doesn't belong to you."

"But there's no one around," said Jim, sulking.

"No matter. There must be people living nearby; otherwise this raft wouldn't be here." He squinted at the forest but could not discover a house.

"Heck!" he said. "There must be a path some-where."

"There is an opening over there," said Peggy, who had very good eyes. "Perhaps it's a path."

Ralph walked toward the opening. A narrow path led into the forest. It was made of concrete and had a white line down the center and rather deep ditches on either side. Inside the forest, the path curved sharply so that the children could not see what was ahead. It was still quite dim in the woods, and Peggy and Jim hesitated.

"Do we want to go in?" asked Jim, looking wor-ried.

"You bet," said Ralph, gleefully rubbing his hands. "There's nothing doing on the beach."

Once more Ralph took the lead, and Peggy and Jim followed timidly. The path was so narrow that they had to walk in single file. Fortunately, the trees did not grow very close to the path; otherwise they would have been obliged to crawl because of the many low branches.

"Why is there a white line in the middle of the path?" Peggy wanted to know.

"No idea," called Ralph, without turning around. "It looks like a highway in miniature. But everything seems to be crazy in this crazy country."

"Everything is bewitched!" said Jim crossly. His wet sneakers were full of sand and his feet hurt. Every so often, the path curved sharply and then it zigzagged up a hill.

Peggy started to complain again. "If I don't get something to eat pretty soon, I shall die of hunger!" she declared.

"Now don't give up," said Ralph, trying to cheer her on. "We're bound to find people soon."

"If there are people here, we'd hear something," said Jim.

"The people are asleep," said Ralph. "The sun hasn't come up yet."

"Then we won't get breakfast for a long time," said Peggy with a groan.

"We'll wake them up," said Ralph reassuringly. He stopped and listened intently. "Quiet! I think I hear something."

Now, Peggy and Jim heard it too. From somewhere far away came the baying of dogs, the honking of cars, and the rat-tat-tat of motorcycles. People seemed to be shouting at each other in anger. The sound came from beyond the hill. Gradually, the noise grew fainter as if more distant.

"Let's go; those are people!" Ralph called excitedly.

The children ran up the hill, but it took them a while before they reached the top. When they got to the top, they froze in their tracks. Below them stretched a long valley over which the rising sun was casting its early rays. It was dotted with small square fields and meadows. Here and there lay houses and barns surrounded by fruit orchards and vegetable gardens. At a point where the concrete path leading into the valley merged with several country roads, there was a village with a square in the center. In the middle of the square stood a church, and beyond it they could see a railway station. From there, railroad tracks ran along wooded slopes and disappeared into a canyon between two hills. The windowpanes of the houses, reflecting the sun, glowed crimson red. The railroad tracks glistened like freshly polished silver.

It was a peaceful sight. The church spire was no higher than a dunce cap, the houses no larger than dollhouses, and the railroad tracks no wider than an ironing board. Neither man nor beast could be seen anywhere.

4

Something Very Small

"Well, I'll be a fried kangaroo," said Ralph, perplexed. "Why are the houses so small?"

"And look," called Peggy, "even the gardens are tiny. And the fruit trees!"

Jim didn't say anything; he just kept his mouth open in complete amazement. Silently, the children looked down upon the valley. The houses looked like toys. The small meadows sparkled in their fresh green. The fields were brown and the roofs were red. In the early morning sun, the church tower cast a long shadow across the square.

"That's the way things must seem from an airplane," said Ralph, and looked around as though he wanted to make sure that he really was not in a plane. But they were still standing on top of a hill no higher than three hundred feet.

"I know! I know!" Peggy cried suddenly.

"What do you know?" Ralph asked tensely.

"Jim, do you remember the letter Uncle Henry sent us from Holland at Christmastime?" asked Peggy.

"It was too long to read it all," replied Jim, sulking.

"But I told you all about it. He wrote that in Holland they had a miniature town just for children."

"What is miniature?" Jim interrupted her.

"Miniature is something very small which normally is much bigger," Ralph instructed him.

"I see," murmured Jim, not having understood a word. "And why do they have such a miniature town?"

"For the children," Peggy continued. "It's an exhibition. You pay to get in and then you are allowed to look at everything. Someday, when we visit Uncle Henry in Holland, he will take us there."

"Are we in Holland?" asked Jim.

"How can you be so stupid?" cried Peggy, in despair. "Of course we're not in Holland! The people here just built the same thing for their children."

"But everything is so small!" objected Ralph. "The fields, the roads, the tracks, and even the telegraph poles."

"That's why it is all for children," insisted Peggy obstinately.

"But if it is an exhibition, somebody should be here to guard it," said Ralph, still doubtful.

"We heard people a little while ago, even dogs."

"But now there isn't a thing in sight," said Ralph, "not even the tail of a dog."

"But it's Sunday today. Perhaps they all went on trips."

"Well, if that's the case, good-bye, breakfast," said Ralph with a funny grunt. "Tighten your belts. I've already got mine in the last hole."

Peggy and Jim for once were too excited to think of eating. They wanted to look at everything at once. Peggy could no longer restrain herself. She ran down into the valley. Like a little dog, Jim chased after her.

"Wait for me!" he yelled. "I'm coming with you."

Reluctantly, Ralph followed. He wondered why there was no one around and no really big house to be seen. When he got to the foot of the hill, Peggy and Jim were stamping through fields and meadows surrounded by matchlike fences. They were heading for a farmhouse.

"Stay back!" shouted Ralph. "Not on the fields! You're trampling down everything. Something has been planted there."

Peggy and Jim returned, a bit embarrassed.

"We didn't see any plants," Peggy explained apologetically.

"You're wrong," said Ralph. "They're so tiny you'd better stay here."

Once again they proceeded in single file along the path. Nearby, a rooster crowed timidly, and they stopped in astonishment.

"There must be chickens around," said Ralph.

They looked for a long while, but when they could not discover any, they walked on. After a turn in the road, they came upon the first houses of the village. This was the beginning of a street in miniature, with sidewalks and electric streetlamps. The street was wider than the path, which gave the children more room. The tiny bulbs in the streetlamps were burning, much to their amazement.

"They must have forgotten to turn them off," said Ralph.

"Probably the exhibition is also open in the evening," suggested Peggy.

On one side of the street, a row of houses extended to the square. But because the houses were surrounded by gardens with flower beds and shade trees, the children could not get close enough to inspect them. They could only look down on the rooftops and chimneys, which made them feel like giants in a fairy tale. But on the other side of the street, where there still were open fields, there was a filling station. It was exactly as small as the houses and had two gasoline pumps painted blue and white. A round sign with the word "Liliko" painted in red letters dangled from an iron pole. Between the gas pumps there was a rack with very small tires and many oil cans. The cans too had the word "Liliko" painted on them. Behind the gas station was a garage. There were no cars in it, but tools were strewn about just as in a real garage; screwdrivers, car jacks, grease pumps, hammers, pliers, drills, and the like. Right next to the garage was a repair shop. Inside, a car stood on a lift. Apparently it was in the process of being repaired, as the hood was raised and the engine had been taken apart. One could even see the tiny valves and cylinders.

The garage and gas station were, in every detail, such faithful copies of real ones that the children were completely captivated.

"They thought of everything," said Ralph admiringly. "There's even a water can next to the pumps, just as it should be." He stooped to look into it and called, "There's even a little water in it. Now, how do you like that?"

Peggy stared at the sign. "What does 'Liliko' mean?" she wanted to know.

"Don't you know that real gas stations always

have a sign advertising the kind of gas they sell?" Ralph said.

"How sweet!" exclaimed Peggy, enchanted, although at home she never paid any attention to filling stations.

Jim was beside himself with excitement. He kneeled down at one of the pumps, turned the crank, and took off the hose, which was about as thick and as long as the stick of a lollipop. There was a clicking noise. Behind the glass pane, numbers started to tick off and a bright fluid spilled onto the pavement.

"Take your hands off it!" Ralph hissed at him.

"It smells like gas!" said Jim.

Ralph grabbed the hose from Jim and hung it back on the hook by the side of the pump. The pump stopped running.

"Lucky nobody saw you," he said, anxiously looking around.

Jim took advantage of this moment to try to crawl into the repair shop. But the door was too small and his head got stuck. Ralph pulled him out by the seat of his pants and ordered him to get up immediately.

"These aren't toys," he said emphatically. "They are just to look at."

"You're always scared," said Jim petulantly, and gave him an angry look out of the corner of his eye.

"If you don't like it, you can manage on your own," said Ralph and left him.

Meanwhile, Peggy had reached the square and called excitedly, "Come here, it's fantastic!"

Around the square stood a group of houses with gardens in the rear. Most of them had only one floor, but a few had two. The square seemed quite spacious and was crisscrossed by narrow, deep canals spanned by tiny bridges. The reason for these canals mystified the children because there was no water in them. The ivy-covered church looked old and was surrounded by well-kept lawns. On one side was a cemetery with tiny tombstones. The church tower was at least three times taller than the biggest house in the village. Even so, the children could easily touch the top of the spire with their fingers.

Ralph bent down and looked in through the stained-glass windows. The slanting rays of the sun shone upon a row of pews and on the altar with the organ behind it. The rest of the interior was hidden in the dim light of the early morning. Suddenly, the church bell began to ring, and Ralph straightened up with a start. "The clock runs," he said, dumbfounded. "It's half past six."

But Peggy and Jim had left him a while ago. On their hands and knees, they were crawling around the square to look at the houses. Peggy stopped in front of one and opened and shut the front door. Then she rang the doorbell. Inside a bell sounded, which amused her so much that she kept on ringing.

Across the square, Jim was crawling along a row of shops. He discovered a pharmacy, a bakery, a stationery shop, and a grocery. But in all of them the shutters were closed, so that he could not peek inside. He tried to lift off the roofs, but they were firmly fastened. His little finger happened to get caught in one of the chimneys, and when he pulled it out, it was black.

"There is soot in the chimney," he said with a grin. He wiped the soot off on his pants and crawled on. At the corner of a street there was an inn called "The Golden Pee Wee." Opposite the inn was a bank. Behind the inn was a terrace with tables and chairs. The tables were covered with red-and-white-checked tablecloths. Strung between two trees in the garden hung a swing. Jim flipped it, and it got caught in the branches of the trees. When he tried to pull it back, Jim broke the bar and, with a guilty conscience, looked around for Ralph. But fortunately Ralph had not noticed it. He was kneeling by a canal, concentrating on something. Quickly,

Jim crept on. On the glass door of the bank it said, "Mildendo Savings Bank." The lettering was so tiny that he could hardly read it. There was not much of interest here, but next to the bank was a particularly pretty building. He looked inside.

"Here's a school!" he yelled. He could see benches and desks, the teacher's platform, and a blackboard on the wall. There was some writing on the blackboard. He tried to decipher it, but the writing was even smaller than that on the bank door.

"Come here! Come here!" cried Peggy with such delight that Ralph and Jim instantly ran over to her. She was lying on her stomach in front of a two-story house, with her nose literally glued to the windows of the ground floor.

"Are there dolls in it?" Jim shouted before he got there.

"No!" shouted Peggy. "But it's divine."

"What do you see? Let me look!" cried Jim breathlessly, and tried to pull her back.

But Peggy shook him off and refused to move.

"It has most elegant pieces of furniture inside," she reported, "heaps of armchairs and a leather couch and a bookshelf with books. And over there is a telephone. There's even a television set in the corner. And, oh dear, how cute! On the table there's a tiny black cat made of velvet. She is staring at me. She looks as though she were alive. Help!" she suddenly yelled, jumped up, and held her hand to her mouth.

"What's the matter with you?" asked Ralph.

"The cat," Peggy whispered, aghast.

"What about the cat?" asked Ralph, startled.

"She . . . she . . . humped her back and hissed at me," said Peggy.

5

A Tea Cozy Has No Tail

"Are you sure you saw right?" asked Ralph.

"Oh, yes, she humped her back and hissed at me and her fur was all bristling!"

Ralph kneeled down and looked inside the room. On the table stood a tea cozy and breakfast dishes that had been used. There was no sign of a cat. He got up and gave Peggy a suspicious look.

"There is nothing but a tea cozy on the table," he said, smiling.

"Ha, ha, Peggy thought the tea cozy was a cat!" Jim jeered.

"A tea cozy has no tail," Peggy protested angrily.

"Well, how big was the cat, then?" asked Ralph dubiously.

"As big as my thumb," said Peggy, nodding eagerly and showing him her thumb. "Perhaps she ran away and hid."

Just to make sure, Ralph looked into the second floor.

"That's strange," he called, perplexed.

"What's strange? Let me have a look too," Jim pleaded.

"It's a beautiful bedroom," reported Ralph, "but very untidy. The beds are unmade and the closets wide open. In the back is a chest with all the drawers pulled out. There are clothes lying all over the place, even on the floor."

"Do you see the cat?" asked Peggy.

Ralph got up and, with a groan, rubbed his knees. The pavement was very hard.

"I don't understand why the room is so messy," he said.

"Well, it's supposed to look as if people lived in it," said Peggy.

"But most people don't throw their clothes on the floor," Ralph said austerely.

"The cat may have done it."

"I wish you'd forget about that cat. No cats are that small."

Peggy went into a sulk.

Meanwhile, Jim had run ahead. "There's a trunk lying here on the street!" he yelled.

A miniature trunk made of leather was lying on the sidewalk in front of a house. It had burst open,

4 2

and shoes, stockings, nightgowns, and pajamas were strewn all over the pavement. The garments were so tiny, they looked as if they belonged to a small doll. Enthralled, Peggy picked up one of the nightgowns.

"It is made of silk and lace," she said in admiration, "just the kind Aunt Betty wears."

"Why the dickens is all this stuff lying around here?" murmured Ralph. He took off his tropical

helmet and scratched his head. Then the children discovered there were more trunks, chests, crates, and boxes lying on the sidewalk. They had been too excited to pay any attention to them when they first entered the village. Objects were scattered even on the pavement between the canals—empty baby carriages, tied-up bundles, a roll of carpet, with shreds of paper scattered among them.

"I'll be a Chinaman if I know the meaning of all this!" said Ralph.

"Perhaps robbers did it," suggested Jim.

"Robbers have better things to do than to take this doll stuff," growled Ralph.

"They were naughty children!" Peggy declared with conviction. "They played with these things secretly. I'm sure it's strictly forbidden."

Hastily, Ralph put his tropical helmet back on.

"Let's get out of here quickly. Somebody may come and think that we've done it."

They ran down the tiny street toward the wooded hills with the winding railroad tracks. There were fewer houses, and when there were none at all, the street once again led into the narrow concrete path with the white line in the middle that they had followed from the beach. On either side now, there were nothing but small rectangular fields, lawns, and vegetable patches, occasionally intersected by narrow dirt roads leading to isolated farmhouses and barns. The smell of freshly plowed soil and onions filled the air. Tiny sacks, filled almost to bursting, stood on the edge of the road.

"I smell onions," called Jim.

"Oh, if only I could eat an onion now!" exclaimed Peggy. Her stomach was growling like an angry dog.

"And me an ice cream cone," yelled Jim.

The rays of the sun had become considerably warmer, and a light ground fog rose from the fields.

"I'm exhausted," Peggy called. She stopped and pressed her hand against her ribs.

Ralph immediately turned around. "What's the matter?" he asked anxiously.

"I feel weak and awful," she complained, "and I've got a stinging pain in my ribs."

"Something always stings you," said Jim. His feet burned like fire and he felt cross.

"We don't have to run so fast anymore," said Ralph. "The village is way behind us." He too was tired. After all, in the last twenty-four hours they had had nothing to eat or drink and had only slept half the night. Their shirts and trousers still scraped like sandpaper because of the salt and sand in them.

The path led up a small embankment. Next came a small bridge, with a brook flowing beneath it. The wooden bridge pilings were as thin as broomsticks and the railing only a little higher than dominoes. But the brook was a real brook, lustily splashing past polished rocks.

Ralph hesitated. "The bridge looks very fragile," he said suspiciously.

"Fiddlesticks!" said Jim. He slipped by and ran onto the bridge. At once, there was an ominous cracking noise and several of the pilings splintered. Jim jumped back.

"Oh boy!" he said.

"Do you have to break everything?" growled Ralph, looking around nervously. But the whole countryside was as deserted as before.

"How are we going to get across the brook?" asked Jim, with a sheepish grin.

"We'll wade through it," said Ralph with decision.

Peggy ran down to the bank and cupped her hands to drink.

"Don't drink!" shouted Ralph, and jumped down the embankment. "First let me find out if it's safe." He scooped up some water in his helmet and tasted it. "It's okay," he said, and handed it to her. "Here, drink, Peggy. It tastes good."

Peggy started to drink, but then gave the helmet back to him.

"Your helmet doesn't taste very good," she said, turning up her nose. She lay on her stomach and let the water run into her mouth. Jim stuck his whole head into the water. Ralph drained his helmet, then jumped into the middle of the brook and sat down between two boulders. The water splashed over him.

"Why do you do that?" Peggy asked, surprised.

"Laundry day," said Ralph. "This will take the salt out of our clothes."

"Oh, great," cried Peggy and waded over to him. She sat down next to Ralph and squealed, "It's icy!"

The first thing Jim did was to take his shoes off and shake out the sand. Then he cautiously dipped his big toe into the water. After some hesitation, he sat down in a shallow pool near the bank because there the water was much warmer. When they had bathed, the children stretched out in a meadow on the opposite shore and dried themselves in the sun. They began to feel better. Peggy sat up, squeezed the water out of her hair and started to sing gaily:

> Over in the meadow
> In the sand
> In the sun
> Lived an old mother turtle
> And her little turtle one.

"What kind of song is that?" asked Ralph. "I never heard it before."

He was lying on his back dreamily squinting into the sun.

"My grandmother Gertrude taught it to me when she visited us," Peggy said. "That was a long time ago. My grandmother's American. She lives near Philadelphia. That's a big city in the United States."

"I know," mumbled Ralph. "It's a neat song but right now I'd rather have breakfast. Seven fried eggs, lots of coffee, and a dozen rolls."

"I don't like coffee," said Jim. "I want some hot chocolate."

"Daddy always drinks three cups of coffee for breakfast," said Peggy quietly. She was thinking of her parents and feeling sad. "Our poor parents. If only they knew that we are still alive!"

Ralph sat straight up. "We'll send them a telegram," he said boldly.

"A telegram?" cried Peggy and Jim in surprise.

Jim looked at him in admiration. "Would you really dare send a telegram?"

"Why not?" said Ralph casually. "Nothing could be simpler."

But, as it turned out, it wasn't as simple as he thought.

6

Somebody Waved

"Do you know how to send a telegram?" asked Peggy.

"It's a cinch," said Ralph. "Once I was with my father when he sent one. You take a blank, fill it out, and hand it to the official. That's all there is to it."

"But, do you have money?" asked Peggy.

Ralph was perplexed. "Shucks, I don't."

"Neither do we," said Peggy dejectedly.

Gloomily, Ralph stared in front of him. This did not make him look very inspired. The brook gurgled between the boulders as though it were making fun of him.

"Perhaps we could borrow some," proposed Peggy.

"That's it," called Ralph cheerfully. "After all, we are shipwrecked. Anybody should be willing to lend us some."

"And we'll surely return it," said Peggy with honest determination.

"What are you going to say in the telegram?" asked Jim.

"Something as brief as possible so it won't cost much," said Ralph. His parents had taught him to be economical.

"But what?" Peggy wanted to know.

"Let me think," growled Ralph, feeling irritated. He wrinkled his forehead and pondered.

"How about 'All well, send money'?"

"That is very short," said Jim, disappointed.

"Well, we could add 'Many regards and kisses, Peggy, Jim, and Ralph.' "

" 'Many regards and kisses' may be too expensive," suggested Peggy.

"Well, then, only 'many regards.' "

"No, just 'many kisses,' " said Peggy. She loved her parents very much.

"Where will they send the money to?" asked Jim. "We have no idea where we are."

"I hope we're finally going to find out," said Ralph.

They were about to lie down again when they heard an airplane approaching. Excitedly, they jumped up.

"A plane! A plane! I can see it!" called Peggy. She pulled off her cap and waved furiously.

"Those are our parents!" shouted Jim, and gleefully turned cartwheels across the field.

The airplane was only a shiny dot in the dark blue sky. It was flying extremely high.

"It's a helicopter," said Ralph. "It has no wings."

They waved and waved, but the helicopter only went higher, swung, and disappeared inland.

Furiously, Jim pounded his fists on the grass. "Why didn't they see us?" he cried.

"The plane was from here," said Ralph.

"You couldn't possibly know that," cried Jim.

"I can too. They weren't looking for anybody; otherwise they would have flown much lower. That helicopter was at least thirty thousand feet up. That's how small it looked."

"And I was so glad," murmured Peggy. She had to hold onto herself in order not to cry.

Ralph cleared his throat. "No use whining and gnashing our teeth. We'd better start walking again."

"But my feet hurt," complained Jim.

"Then you'll have to sit here and wait until we come back for you."

Jim didn't like that, and he put on his shoes at once.

"I must look like a witch," said Peggy. "What will people think of me? If only I had a comb!" In vain, she groped in her bag. "My hair's a mess."

"We'll also borrow a comb," Ralph promised her.

"Really?"

"Cross my heart," said Ralph. Peggy smiled gratefully.

They scampered up the embankment to the path and continued to walk. The bathing had refreshed them, but now they were hungrier than ever. A wind had sprung up, and from behind the range of hills rose thick, grayish clouds. The children reached the forest that covered the slopes. The trees were just as low as those on the beach but not quite as thick. Almost immediately, they came to a fork in the road and Ralph did not know whether to continue left or right.

"There is a road sign over there," Peggy murmured faintly.

The road sign was so small that Ralph had overlooked it. He kneeled down squinting, to read the tiny signs. The one pointing to the left said, "To Plips, 1 mile," and below it, "To Mildendo, 3 miles." The one pointing to the right just read, "To the Station."

Ralph jumped up. "Plips, that's the next place,"

he announced cheerfully. "Not far at all, just one mile."

"But I would like to see the station," said Jim.

"We don't have time for that. Let's first try to find people in Plips who can help us."

"But I do want to see the station. Perhaps there will be a locomotive there."

"You wouldn't be allowed to play with it anyway," said Peggy.

"But I want to look at it," Jim insisted obstinately.

"Okay, let him go to the station," said Ralph. "We'll go to Plips for breakfast." Suddenly, he stopped to listen. The soft, clear sound of a train whistle was coming closer and closer. Then deep inside the forest a bell rang shrilly and farther along where the right-hand path turned a bend, two red lights flashed on either side.

"That's a railway crossing," yelled Jim, and took off like a rocket. Peggy and Ralph ran after him. They got there just in time to see the small railway gates being lowered as though by an invisible hand. There was no guard house, nor guard, but the bells still clanged and the caution lights blinked. From the right side of the forest, the whistle blew louder and more menacingly and a miniature train sped toward them. It was a streamliner with many cars of shiny aluminum. It banked with the curve of the track, then righted itself on the straightaway, and, like a streak, pounded past the gates. Fascinated, the children looked down on the curved roofs as the train sped by. Dust and shreds of paper whirled up between the tracks.

"The exhibition must be open after all," said Ralph in surprise. "Otherwise, that little train wouldn't be running."

"What makes it run?" asked Peggy. "After all, there isn't anybody around."

"Electricity," Ralph explained to her. "Didn't you notice that the streetlamps were burning too? It probably runs around the hill in a circle all the time."

Jim was enchanted. "Oh, please, let's wait until it comes around again," he pleaded.

Far down the tracks the train went into a curve and the children got another good look at the engine and the cars. A window was open in the last car and a tiny hand waved from it. Then the train disappeared between the hills.

"Holy mackerel!" stammered Ralph. "What was that? I could have sworn that somebody was waving!"

Peggy's eyes sparkled with excitement. "There

were a lot of tiny people sitting inside," she insisted. "I thought they were dolls."

"That just doesn't exist," murmured Ralph, dumbfounded. "It's impossible."

"I mean it," said Peggy, nodding gravely. "The train was crowded. People were even standing in the aisles."

The locomotive whistled softly somewhere beyond the hill. Ralph suddenly came back to life.

"Come! Quick! Quick! I've got to have another look at the train. We must have made a mistake."

They ran down the path toward the slope and discovered that it led through a tunnel. Helplessly, they stood in front of it. The entrance to the tunnel was no higher than the opening of a doghouse.

"We can't squeeze through that," said Ralph in disgust.

"Perhaps we can climb up the hill through the forest," proposed Peggy. "The trees are not so close."

"Let's go! It's worth a try," cried Ralph, "but mind the low branches so that you won't hurt your eyes."

"Yes!" cried Peggy. Like a goat, she went scampering up the hill.

Jim was close behind her. Ralph could not follow as quickly because he was taller and heavier. A few times he got stuck between two tree trunks and had to turn back to find an easier way. His helmet kept sliding down on his nose, and he finally carried it in his teeth.

Ralph could no longer see Peggy and Jim. But he could hear them breaking off branches to clear their way. Suddenly, Peggy cried, half choked, "Ralph! Ralph! Ralph!"

Then there was silence as though she had fainted. Frantically, Ralph squeezed through a few last trees. At last, he saw Peggy and Jim. They were lying at the edge of the forest looking down without saying a word.

"What's the matter?" called Ralph. Still silent, Peggy pointed down the slope. Quickly, Ralph crept up to her. He too was speechless.

Below them, stretching as far as the horizon, unfolded a country of rolling hills. The shadows of drifting clouds moved lazily across the fields. The little streamliner was just then hustling between two hills, and the children could only see the tops of the cars. Through gaps in the overcast, the sun shone brilliantly on the abundant fields and mead-ows. The whole countryside seemed to be studded with villages, hamlets, and farms, all connected by a network of country roads. Beyond a river with several bridges there was a town with many church towers, and toward the southwest, a big city appeared on the far horizon. Tall buildings and even a few skyscrapers rose from its center. Many factories stood on the outskirts. Their smokestacks looked like straws standing on end.

It was a world of miniatures. Nothing was much bigger than a toy. The skyscrapers seemed no taller than thirty feet. The highways were the same width as the path with the white line in the center.

Only one expressway was somewhat wider. Bypassing all the villages, it ran in a straight line toward the big city. On each side of a narrow, deep ditch, there were three car lanes. Not far from where the children were lying on the hill, a long column of tiny vehicles was trundling toward the southwest. Passenger cars, buses, and trucks with and without trailers were creeping along bumper-to-bumper. Between the columns there were many motorcycles. The children once more heard the sound of dogs barking. The air was filled with the roar and the backfiring of motors and heavy with the smell of exhaust fumes. All the cars were crammed to capacity. The trucks and buses were piled high with trunks, bundles, crates, and boxes. A helicopter hovered over the entire scene. It was not very high and looked no bigger than an old-fashioned coffee grinder.

Suddenly, the sirens started to wail again.

7

It's No Fun to Be a Giant

The sirens wailed for at least five minutes, and the long column of vehicles began to gather speed. Those in the rear blew their horns ceaselessly to hurry those in front. The helicopter hovered over them like a sparrow watching its fledglings. Fascinated, the children looked on in silence.

Peggy was the first to speak again. "We're in a land of dwarfs!" she cried out in delight.

"Dwarfs are much taller," said Jim ponderously. "I know all about dwarfs."

"Then they are dwarfs of dwarfs," insisted Peggy.

Ralph was completely dumbfounded.

"Fantastic," he murmured, and shook his head in amazement.

Now Peggy began to wonder. "Perhaps this is only a dream," she said nervously.

"But we can't all dream the same thing at the same time," said Ralph.

"We have suddenly become giants!" Jim cried, completely rattled.

"If we had suddenly grown into giants, you would have busted out of your pants a long time ago," observed Ralph.

Startled, Jim stared at his pants. They still fitted him although they were not as clean as the day before.

"The cat hissed at me after all!" said Peggy, looking at Ralph defiantly.

"Fantastic!" Ralph groaned again.

"And somebody really did wave from the train," said Jim.

"It was a little girl with pigtails and red ribbons," Peggy added quickly.

Silently, Ralph looked down on the expressway. The tiny little cars were just moving up an incline. They were not very far away, at the most nine hundred feet, but, as they were all so tiny, they looked miles away.

"Why are they all moving away from us?" asked Peggy.

"Perhaps they are fleeing," suggested Ralph.

"But we mean them no harm," said Peggy, perplexed.

"How would they know? Giants are giants. What would you do if suddenly three giants turned up at home and walked toward you?"

"I'd quickly hide," said Peggy, frightened.

"There, you see?" said Ralph smugly.

"Shouldn't we run after them and call to them that we mean them no harm?"

"No, no, no, certainly not, that would only scare them more and possibly cause an accident. But this way we will get nothing to eat."

"I can just imagine what their food is like," Jim hinted dejectedly.

"They probably eat grains of corn," said Peggy.

"But these people are quite up-to-date," said Ralph. "They have cars, trains, helicopters, and even television. With all that, they wouldn't be eating grains of corn. They aren't baby chicks."

"But they're almost as small as baby chicks," said Peggy anxiously. She looked miserable and hungry.

"I'm sure they'll have something to eat," said Ralph, trying to cheer up Peggy. But he was not so sure himself.

"Do they have hot cocoa?" asked Jim.

"I always drink a lot of milk at home," interrupted Peggy.

"How should I know whether they have cocoa or milk?" said Ralph. "What is far more important, how can we show them that we mean them no harm without running after them?" At a loss, he scratched his head.

"We have to shout," said Peggy.

"No, they wouldn't hear it. They are making too much noise. Wait, I've got it!"

"What?" asked Peggy and Jim tensely.

"We'll wave at them with green twigs," said Ralph happily.

"Why?" wondered Peggy.

"Waving with green twigs means that we are peaceful," declared Ralph. "It is known all over the world. I read that in my books about great explorers."

Hastily, he tore off branches, left and right. They were thick with leaves and he gave two to Peggy and Jim.

"Now we're the savages," said Jim, grinning, and started to wave the twigs.

The trees were so low that they could not stand up, so they slid down a steep, grassy bank. They landed on a fairly large field and waved at the cars with their branches, but apparently the fleeing crowd did not pay any attention to them. The cars only moved at a faster pace.

"These people haven't read your books," said Peggy.

"They just didn't see us," Ralph replied with irritation. "This field is below the level of the highway."

To the left of them was a lake surrounded by a number of bungalows. On the right, the narrow path emerged from the tunnel. A ramp led to the entrance of the expressway. In front of it was a concrete plaza.

"Let's climb up the bank to the plaza," said Ralph. "From there, the people will see us better."

But when they reached the top, the cars had just disappeared behind a knoll. All they saw was the helicopter.

"Now they're gone," said Peggy, annoyed.

"We'll just have to wait until they appear again," said Ralph.

"That can take a long time. They were driving terribly slowly."

"That's only the way it seems to you because they are so small."

"But I can't stand up any longer," said Peggy, "and I don't want to sit down on the hard ground."

Across the expressway stood something made of concrete resembling a stone bench. It had a flat roof, and under it, evenly spaced, were six little booths made of glass and aluminum. Ralph tested the roof with his hands.

"It's quite safe to sit on it," he said. "It will

certainly support us." He stepped over it and sat down so that he could look at the expressway. Peggy and Jim sat down next to him.

"Oh, that feels good!" said Peggy, taking a deep breath.

Since their unhappy trip on the raft, it was the first time that she could sit and dangle her legs again.

"It's no fun to be a giant all of a sudden," she added with a sigh.

"I think it's great!" said Jim enthusiastically. "Now I can lick everybody!"

Ralph was furious. "Just lay off," he said threateningly.

Startled, Jim kept silent.

"Where are we going to sleep?" asked Peggy. "We'll never fit into any of those houses."

"Outdoors," said Ralph blithely. He was not worried in the least. His father used to drive cattle over great distances in the north of Australia. A few times he had taken Ralph along. On those occasions they had to camp out at night. "After all, we slept quite well in the rubber raft out on the ocean."

"Not me," said Jim.

"But what shall we do when it rains?" asked Peggy. "We'll get wet all over again." Anxiously, she looked up. Clouds were gathering in the sky.

"Why didn't you bring your umbrella along?" said Jim in a mocking voice. He bent down and eagerly looked under the roof. "What are these little houses for?"

"No idea!" Ralph shrugged his shoulders.

Peggy knew. "They are tollbooths," she said. "My friend Julia went to live in America, and she wrote me that when you go on one of those super-highways, you have to pay all the time."

"Do we have to pay too?" asked Jim.

"But we're walking," said Peggy.

"More of those shreds of paper lying around," said Ralph, and picked one up. "This is a news-paper," he said, perplexed.

"Let me see! Let me see!" called Peggy and Jim excitedly, sidling up to him.

It was a real newspaper except that it was no larger than a big stamp. But the headlines were very big. The children put their heads together and read:

THE PLIPS MORNING POST

EXTRA! EXTRA!

GIANTS HAVE LANDED!

THREE GIANTS HAVE LANDED ON THE BEACH OF

ALLENBECK

———

The entire population of the east coast evacuating
State of emergency in Plips
Cabinet meets in Mildendo
Proclamation by Queen imminent
All officials to remain at their posts!

The children could not read what followed because the print was too small.

"They are really fleeing from us," said Ralph. "That is why everything is so deserted."

"They even have a queen," exclaimed Peggy in admiration. "I wonder whether she too is so tiny."

"I'm sure she's the tiniest of them all," said Jim.

"Here comes the helicopter!" cried Ralph, anxiously.

The helicopter must have spotted them, for it flew directly toward them.

Peggy and Ralph jumped up and waved their twigs. Peggy could not contain herself and yelled: "We won't hurt you! We won't hurt you! All we want is something to eat."

The noise of the propeller grew louder and louder. The helicopter came nearer and nearer, and they could see two small men inside the plastic blister. Just when it was quite low over them, Jim yanked his gun from his shoulder, aimed it at the two men and, yelling "tack, tack, tack," pretended to shoot at them.

Quickly, the helicopter rose and flew off.

Ralph was speechless with rage. "Are you completely crazy!" he yelled, and knocked the gun aside.

"They were going to attack us," stuttered Jim.

"Nonsense!" cried Ralph. "Probably they wanted to call something to us."

Peggy too was furious. "If they had come any closer, they might have heard me in spite of the noise of the propeller. Now you've spoiled everything!"

"You always pick on me," Jim protested.

"You're impossible!" said Peggy heatedly.

"Hand me the gun at once," ordered Ralph.

"What are you going to do with it?" asked Jim suspiciously.

"We've got to get rid of this gun," said Ralph, and grabbed it away from him. "How could they know it was only a toy?" He looked around for a place to hide it.

"My gun, give me back my gun!" whined Jim.

"Don't act like a baby," scolded Peggy. "Daddy will give you a new one for Christmas."

"But I don't want a new one," cried Jim, and stamped his feet.

Ralph walked up the expressway a short distance

to the beginning of the ditch separating the lanes. Jim ran after him. Peggy followed behind him.

"Quit acting that way," she called.

Ralph wanted to put the gun into the ditch, but it would not fit. Suddenly, someone nearby said: "Let me have that thing; I'll keep it for you." Startled, they looked around.

On their right near the highway was a small vegetable patch in front of a freshly mowed hayfield. Further away they could see wheat fields, farmhouses, and barns. On the hayfield, as though it had suddenly sprung from the ground, stood a miniature tractor hitched to a wagon piled high with hay. The motor was clanking and white puffs of smoke rose from the exhaust pipe. On the tractor sat a man no bigger than a small doll. His white hair flowed in the wind. He wore overalls and smoked a pipe. The children could smell the tobacco. The man shut off his motor and with a friendly nod said: "So you are the terrible giants! Greetings!"

"How do you do?" murmured Peggy and, without realizing it, made a curtsy.

"The helicopter would have done you no harm," said the man. His voice was not very loud, but the children had no trouble in understanding him.

"They were only the press photographers of the *Mildendo News*. I reckon they took pictures of you for their newspaper. What are you doing with those tree trunks?"

"We waved these twigs to show that we were peaceful," said Ralph.

"Twigs you call them? To us they are tree trunks. You'd better throw them away, else the folks will think you want to kill them."

The children dropped the twigs at once.

"Aren't you afraid of us?" asked Peggy, staring down at the tiny man with eyes wide open.

"No longer. But I fairly died of fright when I suddenly saw you slide down the big mountain." With his pipe, he pointed toward the small hill where the children had lain below the trees.

"I quickly hid in the wheat field. Then I listened to what you were saying to each other. Seems to me you're quite harmless."

"We really won't hurt you," said Peggy hastily.

"Reckon you're children; is that right?"

"Oh, yes," said Peggy with a deep sigh.

"Kind of big for children, I daresay," said the man, shaking his head. "Where you from?"

"From Australia," said Ralph timidly. He was often timid when he spoke with adults.

"Australia?" repeated the man slowly. "Never heard of it."

"But Australia is very well known," said Peggy modestly.

"Not here. Now tell me, how did you happen to get here? It's been two hundred and fifty years since a giant managed that."

"We're shipwrecked," said Ralph.

"Shipwrecked! You don't say! The whole country is in a turmoil because of you."

"I beg your pardon," said Ralph, clearing his throat. "Exactly where are we?"

"You are in Lilliput," said the man and, with a nail, started to clean out his pipe.

The children were speechless.

8

Times Have Changed

A gust of wind swept across the wheat field, bending the stalks. In the distance, one could hear the drone of the helicopter and the honking of the cars. A few scattered raindrops splashed on Ralph's and Jim's helmets, but the children didn't notice them. Bewildered, they just stared at the little man.

"But didn't you know that?" he asked in astonishment.

"But Lilliput is a fairy tale," said Peggy in confusion.

"Oh, ho, I beg your pardon!" the man said, a bit offended. "Where did you get that from?"

"I read *Gulliver's Travels*," stuttered Peggy.

"That old Gulliver! How do you like that! So he even wrote a book about us! Well, well, why not. Wouldn't have minded reading it myself."

"But can you read English?" asked Peggy, even more confused.

"I talk English, don't I? Would seem natural that I could read it too. Haven't you yet found out that we speak English here?"

Again the children were dumbfounded. The headlines were all in English, but up to now they had taken it for granted. Now they realized that it wasn't so natural after all.

"But the Lilliputians didn't speak English, did they?" asked Peggy. She knew *Gulliver's Travels* almost by heart.

"Correct, correct," said the man. "This Gulliver had been gone for a long while . . . wait a minute, how long ago was that? That's right, in the year 1751 the Council of the Island made it a law by a two-thirds majority. Since then, English has been the language of our country. Our old language was very cumbersome. Especially the double-accusative. English is much more practical. Gulliver, in those days, learned our language and we his. Only the 'th' was a bit of a problem in the beginning."

"You know a lot," said Peggy admiringly.

"Didn't go to school for nothing. What you've learned you've learned. Never can hurt."

"We go to school too," said Jim.

The man eyed him from top to bottom, which took a fairly long time.

"Must be a mighty big building, your school," he said with a grin.

Ralph cleared his throat. "I beg your pardon, I always thought the Lilliputians ran around in knickers and buckled shoes, and shot bows and arrows." He once had borrowed *Gulliver's Travels* from Peggy.

"How do you like that! That was two hundred and fifty years ago," said the man laughingly. "What do you take us for? Do you think we've been asleep during all those years? We kept up with the times. Unfortunately," he added a bit nostalgically, "almost wish the times hadn't changed. The prices nowadays! And the automobile traffic! What is it all coming to? By the way, my name is Hank Krumps. I own the farm here." With his pipe, he described a vague circle.

"Pleased to meet you," said Peggy politely. She was well brought up. "My name is Peggy. The big boy is our friend Ralph. The small one is my brother Jim."

"You call him small?" asked Mr. Krumps, amused. "He's as tall as a flagpole. And I guess you're a girl, unless I'm mistaken. Eh?"

"Oh, yes," said Peggy proudly.

"No offense," said Mr. Krumps. "At first, I took you for a boy too. Reckon it must have been on account of the shorts. Say, do you suppose you could make yourself a little smaller? I've got a kink in my neck from having to look up to you all the time."

"Would you mind if we stretched out on your field?" asked Peggy. "Then we won't be so tall anymore."

"All right with me, but just take care that you don't step on the onion patch. Otherwise, there'll be nothing but onion juice left."

"We love onions," said Peggy to be polite.

The children stepped over and lay down in the field in front of the tractor.

They propped their heads up on their hands, and that way their eyes were about level with Mr. Krumps. They could see now that he was very old. He had many creases in his face, but his eyes were blue and cheerful. He also was very sunburned.

"Great Scott!" said Mr. Krumps. "Close by, you all look mighty sinister."

"Do we really look so frightening?" asked Peggy meekly.

"Those eyes! You hardly would believe it," said Mr. Krumps, shaking his head. "And those noses! It must be a major catastrophe when you get a cold."

"I agree it's awful," said Peggy. "I hate colds." She had hardly finished when she had to sneeze.

She managed to pull out her handkerchief quickly and hold it before her face before she exploded, but even so, Mr. Krumps would have fallen off his tractor if he had not held on.

"Jeepers! I almost got blown off!" he exclaimed. "If you have to sneeze again, give me fair warning, please."

"I'm sorry," Peggy stammered in embarrassment. "Something tickled my nose."

"It's all right," said Mr. Krumps, appeased. "All that fresh hay."

"May I touch the tractor?" asked Jim. During the entire time he had been looking at it longingly.

"Better not," said Mr. Krumps nervously. "It might crumble under your fingers."

"On our farm we have tractors with Diesel motors," said Jim.

"I don't know about them. Diesel motors? Never

heard of them. This here is a three-cylinder Timko. Four gears. Like it a lot. Only the carburetor is liable to gum up. But don't tell me that you giants can have cars. That's impossible."

"We're no giants," said Jim. "You're a dwarf."

Mr. Krumps was not pleased to hear that. "Now, let's put a stop to that," he said gruffly. "I'm not a dwarf. You're much too tall."

"We can't help it," said Peggy apologetically. "At home everybody is tall." She smiled amiably.

Mr. Krumps had quickly regained his good humor. "Well, I always say everything is relative," he said. He seemed very well educated. "When most people are tall, the short ones are called dwarfs, and when most people are short, the tall ones are called giants. Isn't that so?"

Ralph had listened eagerly. "But what do you do when one half is small and the other half big?" he asked. He was fond of pondering such tricky questions.

Laughing, Mr. Krumps raised both hands in protest. "Well, then they just have to toss a coin to see who calls who what," he said.

The children laughed too. They liked Mr. Krumps. If all Lilliputians were that nice, they had nothing to be afraid of.

"We're sorry that all the people have run away from us," said Peggy.

"You can't blame them," said Mr. Krumps. "Immediately after they read the newspaper this morning, my wife and my mother-in-law flew the coop—no team of horses could have held them back. I would have cleared out myself, but I had to bring in the hay. Looks like rain; I've felt a few drops already."

"We've seen the newspaper too," said Ralph, "but unfortunately we couldn't read the small print."

"Well, they wrote the usual stuff," said Mr. Krumps. "The submarine Seahorse, on off-shore patrol, happened to hear you last night on the beach. Four volunteers managed to land in a rubber raft, despite the big surf, and tried to sneak up on you."

"Those were the footprints," murmured Ralph.

"But they couldn't find you, or perhaps they didn't dare come closer. At any rate, they ran to the Coast Guard Station and looked for you with searchlights. Then they immediately sounded the general alarm."

"We heard the sirens," said Peggy.

"The folks from Allenbeck hastily gathered up a few of their belongings. Everything else they just left behind and then they fled helter-skelter. They passed by here a short while ago. They didn't even take time out for breakfast. They locked up the livestock in the barns so that you wouldn't step on them by mistake."

The word breakfast made Peggy pick up her ears.

"What do the Lilliputians eat?" she asked eagerly.

Mr. Krumps looked startled.

"Eat? Why, everything. Meat, fish, vegetables, butter, bread, milk. Why do you ask me?"

"We're starved," said Peggy, embarrassed. "We've had nothing to eat since yesterday. We just drank a bit of water from the brook."

"We can't have that," cried Mr. Krumps resolutely. "I have two sandwiches with me." Out of his overalls he took two tiny packages and unwrapped two sandwiches. They were about the size of aspirin tablets. He scratched his ear thoughtfully. "I'm afraid these two sandwiches won't feed three giants," he said with a worried expression. "Unfortunately, I don't have much at home either. I'm just not equipped for giants."

"Will we have to starve to death?" asked Peggy sadly.

"Tut, tut, tut! No reason to throw the towel into

the ring right away. We Lilliputians have never yet let anyone die of hunger. Not even giants. Mr. Gulliver used to eat well when he was here."

"But how are we going to get anything to eat if the people keep running away from us?" asked Peggy.

"Wait, wait, let me think. I've got it! No! Yes!" Gleefully, he slapped his leg. "I've got it! Call up Pastor Krog immediately. Know him well. Good man, he. I'm sure he didn't scamper off. Neither is he afraid of giants. Just tell him that you are children and don't mean anybody harm and that you're hungry. Don't have to tell him more than that. If I know him, he'll jump right into his car and come here to help you. That's the kind of man Pastor Krog is."

"You mean to say that we could telephone?" asked Ralph in amazement.

"Of course, that's the quickest way. I'm sure you're in a hurry. Aren't you?"

"Oh, yes, of course," said Peggy, nodding. "But where is there a telephone? Couldn't you put in the call for us?"

"I'd be happy to," said Mr. Krumps, and tapped out his pipe. "But unfortunately I'm almost deaf."

The children were confused and said nothing.

"As a boy, I used to love to fool around with firecrackers," Mr. Krumps continued, absentmindedly sucking on his empty pipe. "Didn't have the sense to know better. One of those things went off too soon. Since then, I can't hear a thing."

"B—but you seem to hear *us* all right," said Peggy reluctantly.

"That's because you're giants, with built-in loud-speakers." Mr. Krumps obviously had a sense of humor. He chuckled over his own joke. "I wish all people were giants."

"Where could we telephone?" asked Ralph. Unconsciously, he raised his voice.

"Great Scott! That's a problem, all right. I have a telephone—my wife uses it all day long—but your heads won't fit into my house. But wait. My goodness, I'm an idiot! There are telephones on the expressway. Go to the next filling station. I reckon it's about three hundred feet from here. Quite a distance. Shucks, of course not for you, with your giant steps. Now you'd better get going. But take it easy and don't tread on the onion field. And I must hurry now to get in my hay. High time."

"Doesn't the telephone cost anything in Lilliput?" asked Peggy.

"Sure it does. Nothing is free in this world."

"But we don't have any money," Peggy confessed blushingly.

"Great Scott! You don't have any money either?

Why, of course, how could you! Even if you did have some, I reckon it wouldn't do you much good. Your money must be oversized. Hmmm," he muttered and produced an old-fashioned pouch. He fumbled in it, a bit out of sorts. "Here's a dimeling for you."

He handed Ralph a tiny coin. "With this you can telephone for three minutes. That should be sufficient."

"Thank you very much," said Ralph. "But what is the telephone number of Pastor Krog?"

"Don't know. Call Information. Just ask for Pastor Krog, Kalinda Church in Plips. That should do it."

The children rose. "Many, many thanks for everything," said Peggy glowingly, and held out her hand to him. But she quickly withdrew it because her hand was almost as big as all of Mr. Krumps.

"Think nothing of it," said Mr. Krumps. "It isn't every day that I can do a favor for three giant children." He started up the motor and drove off in a wide circle. But suddenly he turned around and called: "Just leave the gun there. Later on, I will take it to the barn with my tractor. Good luck!"

Then he and his hay wagon disappeared among the fields, and the children could see only the gleam of his white hair.

9

Dial Zero

The children walked up the slope to the expressway to look for the filling station. Peggy and Jim were very tired and walked slowly. By now the sky was covered with a solid layer of clouds. But, fortunately, it was not yet raining. Peggy was glad the sun wasn't shining; her arms and legs were still very sunburned.

"I like Mr. Krumps," she said.

"I didn't want to play with the tractor. I just wanted to honk its horn," said Jim.

"That's all you can think of," growled Ralph.

"Amazing, how well we could understand Mr. Krumps, almost as if he were a real human being," said Peggy.

"Lilliputians *are* real human beings," answered Ralph. "They're just small."

"Frogs are even smaller and you can hear them croak from far away," said Jim.

"Frogs have big bellies—that's why they croak so loud," said Peggy. "Mr. Krumps had no belly."

"I once caught a very thin frog which croaked very loud," insisted Jim.

"The filling station ought to be behind the hill," said Ralph. "I hope we'll see it soon."

Both sides of the expressway were lined with wheat fields, with farmhouses between them, but as the children walked up the incline, they could see at a distance clusters of small and large housing developments. Railroad tracks ran under the expressway and through the forest toward a river, which meandered through the countryside. A number of bridges led into a town. The children could see many tiny automobiles and people moving about the streets and the squares.

"That must be Plips," said Ralph, pointing to the city.

"I think I can see people looking through field glasses, standing on the roofs of their houses," called out Jim.

"They're watching us," said Ralph.

"Why don't they leave too?" asked Peggy.

"They probably think we're bypassing Plips and taking the expressway to that big city farther on. They'll leave all right when we come."

They reached the top of the slope and could see

the filling station lying in a hollow at a road crossing. At a distance, the string of cars again came into view. It had, meanwhile, grown in length and, like an army of ants on the march, was steadily moving toward the big city on the horizon.

The filling station was very large and modern. It was made entirely of glass and concrete and had many rows of pumps. An illuminated sign read "Liliko." Next to the filling station was an attractive restaurant, also designed of glass and concrete. But the one thing the children could not find was a telephone.

"Perhaps it's in the restaurant," said Peggy.

"I don't think so," answered Ralph. "Mr. Krumps knew perfectly well that we wouldn't fit into it."

"Maybe there's somebody inside we could ask."

They kneeled down and peeked inside. There was nobody there. The tables were set with vases of flowers and small baskets with tiny crisp rolls.

"Can we eat the rolls?" asked Peggy.

"No," said Ralph, "that's stealing."

"But we're so hungry!" said Peggy.

"Makes no difference," said Ralph. "Besides, we wouldn't get filled up with these tiny rolls. Pastor Krog surely is going to give us enough to eat."

"If only we knew where the telephone is!"

"There's a small house back there. The telephone might be inside it," said Jim.

Next to the expressway exit, at the point where a concrete strip led into a country road, a little house stood on the lawn. It looked like a miniature guard house. The children ran over to it and Ralph yelled, "Hurray!" It was, indeed, the telephone. A sign on the house even read "Public Telephone."

Unfortunately, it wasn't much larger than a coin bank, and the children had to lie on their stomachs to get near it. Ralph pushed open the door and inside, against the wall, hung a modern dial telephone.

"May I make the call?" asked Jim.

"No," said Ralph. "Peggy has to telephone."

"Me? Why me?" asked Peggy, surprised. "You're much older."

"Your voice is soft and gentle. It won't scare people so much."

"Have I really got a gentle voice?" said Peggy, flattered.

"Mine is very rough," said Ralph, a bit embarrassed.

The truth was, it was not Peggy's gentle voice that made him want her to telephone. He just did not want to admit that he had never before made a call on a pay phone.

"By the way, do you know how to use a tele-phone?" he asked nervously.

"What do you mean?" said Peggy, insulted. "I telephone often."

"But in your house the telephone is entirely different. This is a public one, where you have to put in a coin."

"I have also made calls on pay telephones," said Peggy proudly. "When I was in Sydney, I had to call Aunt Cornelia all the time when Cousin Helen and I went for hikes. She wanted me to ring her every hour so that she knew where we were."

"Good," said Ralph, satisfied. "Here's the money."

He gave her the tiny coin, which he had held firmly in his hand during the entire time.

"Put it in now."

"Before you put it in, you have to take off the receiver," explained Peggy importantly. She stared at the receiver and frowned because it was no larger than a small match. Gingerly, she took it between her thumb and index finger. Luckily, the cord was just long enough to reach outside the door. Peggy held the receiver to her ear and it almost disap-peared into it. Then she held it before her mouth.

"My, the receiver is tiny!" she said helplessly.

"Everything is tiny in Lilliput," said Ralph. "You'll just have to get used to it."

"But how am I to telephone? When I want to hear, I can't talk into it, and when I want to talk, I can't hear."

"Hold it away from you a bit. Then, perhaps you can talk and hear at the same time," suggested Ralph.

Peggy held the receiver away from her. "But I can't hear anything," she said.

"You've got to pay," said Jim.

Peggy put the coin into a slot on the top of the telephone, and the children listened anxiously. There was a buzz in the earpiece.

"Nobody answers. It just buzzes," said Peggy disappointedly.

"But you haven't even dialed," said Jim with a grin.

"I forgot!" said Peggy with a hurt look.

"What do you want me to dial?" she asked Ralph.

"Information, of course," said Ralph impatiently.

"Oh, dear!" called Peggy, "how do you dial it?"

"You dial zero." Jim gloated. "Why don't you let me phone?" Again, he seemed to know better than Peggy.

"No," said Peggy furiously. "I can find the zero." She tried to put her finger into the tiny hole of the dial but it was too big. She was completely stumped.

"My finger has suddenly gotten very thick," she said. "I used to have slender hands. My piano teacher, Miss Martens, always told me so."

"Your fingers aren't thick at all," said Ralph with a grunt. "It's only that the telephone is so tiny. Haven't you got something with a sharp point?"

"Sharp point?" asked Peggy.

"Yes, of course, a pen or something."

"I think I have a bobby pin."

"That's fine, where?"

"In my shoulder bag."

"Well, get it then," said Ralph.

Peggy fumbled in her bag for a while. Finally, she found the bobby pin. She stuck one end into the hole with a zero below it. She turned the dial, and the children again listened tensely. There was a crackling in the earpiece.

"A crackle," said Peggy triumphantly.

"Is that good?" asked Ralph uncertainly.

"Sure that's good," insisted Peggy.

"That isn't good at all," said Jim. "It's a busy signal."

"Hang up and try again," said Ralph.

"But we can't," said Peggy. "If you hang up, you have to pay again, and we don't have any more money."

"If it's busy, you don't have to be afraid to hang up because you get your money back," said Jim.

"Perhaps not in Lilliput," said Peggy sharply.

"Then wait until it stops making that noise," said Jim, chuckling.

"Sure, that's it," said Ralph quickly, as though he had known all the time.

The crackling noise continued for a long time, but then, suddenly, there was a click and a woman's voice squeaked very politely: "A very good day. This is Information."

"Oh boy!" Jim let out. "Somebody's squeaking."

Peggy was so surprised that she just opened her mouth, unable to utter a sound.

10

Mad with Fear

"A very good day. This is Information. This is the Plips exchange," the voice squeaked a bit louder and less politely. "Speak up!"

"A very good day," Peggy breathed as gently as possible.

"Don't yell so," came a squeak. "I can't understand you. What did you say?"

"A very good day," repeated Peggy in confusion.

"If you keep yelling like that, I'll have to hang up," the squeak protested heatedly.

"But I'm not yelling! How can I help it if I'm so big," breathed Peggy.

"Hold your hand in front of the mouthpiece," Ralph hastily whispered to her.

"But you're still screaming!" The squeak sounded shrill.

Peggy held her hand in front of her mouth. "That wasn't me," she stuttered, "that was Ralph."

"It's impossible for me to understand you. Please talk slowly and distinctly. Can I help you?"

"Pastor Krog," said Peggy, encouraged. "Kalinda Church in Plips."

"Sorry, I can't connect you," sounded the squeak regretfully.

"But, Mr. Krumps said we only had to ask for Pastor Krog at the Kalinda Church in Plips, that would be sufficient," said Peggy.

"All circuits are busy because of the general alarm. Only urgent calls are permitted. Is it urgent?"

"It's very urgent," said Peggy quickly. "We haven't eaten since yesterday and have had just a little water to drink from a brook."

"That isn't urgent," declared the squeak.

"But then we have to die of starvation!" cried Peggy in despair.

The lady at Information now seemed a bit more interested.

"Hold the line. I'll give you the Refugee Center."

Peggy looked at Ralph nervously and whispered. "She can't connect me with Pastor Krog. She wants to give me the Refugee Center. What shall I do?"

"I could hear everything," said Ralph. "Talk to the Refugee Center. Possibly they can help us."

"But what shall I tell them?" asked Peggy nervously.

Before Ralph could answer, there was a crackle in the earphone and a squeaky male voice said impatiently: "This is the Refugee Center, Town Hall, Plips."

"A very good day," said Peggy politely. "Mr. Krumps said that we should tell . . ."

"Come to the point," the man interrupted her impatiently. "There are a thousand more people waiting for me. I don't have to tell you what goes on here today. It seems that most of the people are hysterical with fear."

"We don't want to do anything to anybody," protested Peggy. "It's just that we are very hungry. We haven't eaten anything since yesterday. Just a little water from the brook."

"Is that why you're calling me?" the voice squeaked indignantly.

"What?" said Peggy, frightened.

"Haven't you read the paper?"

"Oh yes, but we couldn't read all the fine print."

"That's hardly my fault. Proceed at once to Wiggywack. All evacuees will be fed free of charge by the Green Cross."

"Will we also get something to eat?" asked Peggy hopefully.

"Didn't I tell you that all evacuees will be taken care of by the Green Cross?"

"But we don't know where Wiggywack is."

"What? You don't know where Wiggywack is?" The voice sounded incredulous.

"No," admitted Peggy meekly.

"This hasn't happened to me in all my long life! Don't you know that Wiggywack is the seat of the Island Council? Drive to Mildendo. Wiggywack is a suburb of Mildendo. Ask for Gulliver Street. The food is being distributed in the municipal grade school."

"But it is impossible for us to get in!" moaned Peggy.

"If you don't want to go in, you can eat on the street for all I care," replied the squeaky voice angrily.

"Gladly," said Peggy willingly, "we would love to. What are they having?"

"Coffee and hot dogs."

"Hot dogs?" asked Peggy, alarmed. "How big are they?"

"As big as any hot dogs. You should be glad that you're getting food at all. You can eat until you have your fill."

"That's wonderful!" Peggy cried, thrilled. "Could you tell me quickly how to get to Wiggywack?"

"Where are you now?"

"On the expressway."

"The expressway is long. Exactly where are you on it?"

Ralph whispered to her: "Tell him near Mr. Krumps's."

"I'm to tell you that we're near Mr. Krumps's," said Peggy.

"Mr. Krumps? Who's Mr. Krumps? I don't know any Mr. Krumps."

"Mr. Krumps is a tiny man on a tractor," Peggy explained eagerly. "He smokes a pipe and is almost deaf. Otherwise, he would have telephoned for us."

"That still doesn't tell me where you are. Now, do you or don't you want to give me that information?"

Ralph whispered to her: "Tell him where the mountains are."

"Where the mountains are, I'm to tell you," repeated Peggy dutifully.

"What? You're that far back? Your car must have broken down. What is your position?"

"On our stomachs," said Peggy.

"Oh, good heavens!" squeaked the man, alarmed. "Why didn't you tell me that right away? Are you hurt? Let me see whether I can send an ambulance at once. It will be difficult . . ."

"We're not hurt," said Peggy. "All I have is a sunburn on my arms and legs and Jim's feet ache."

"Is that why you're lying on your stomach?" asked the man in amazement.

"Oh, no," said Peggy. "We're only on our stomachs because the telephone is so low."

"How? What?" exploded the squeaky voice. "The telephone is so low? Are you trying to be funny? I shall have to report your name. Who is this talking?"

"My name is Peggy," she said timidly. "Ralph is our friend. Jim is my little brother."

"Little brother? Are you children?" asked the man, surprised.

"Oh, yes!" said Peggy with a sigh. "We really don't want to do anybody any harm. We are . . ."

"What are you doing on the highway?" asked the man sternly.

"We're telephoning," said Peggy.

"Are you alone?"

"We're all alone. Everybody is running away from us."

"Why? Where are your parents?"

"Our parents don't know where we are. We would have liked to send them a telegram, but we didn't have any money . . ."

"I see, you've run away from your parents," the man interrupted her again.

"Oh, no," said Peggy, shocked. "We'd never do such a thing. We got blown away by the wind . . ."

The squeaky voice literally choked. "You brazen child! How dare you! In this fateful hour of national emergency you indulge in practical joking. This is incredible! Don't you know that three giants have invaded us? I dare you to call again! If you do, I'll send the police after you at once!"

"But we're the giants!" yelled Peggy, close to tears. The man had already hung up.

"He scolded me and hung up," complained Peggy. She was completely dejected.

"You should have told him right away that we are the giants," said Ralph accusingly.

"I thought he would know!" Peggy objected hotly. Furiously, she put back the receiver.

"How on earth would he know?" Ralph scolded her. "After all, he can't see through the telephone!"

"Why didn't you do the telephoning?" screamed Peggy.

"I certainly would have if I'd known that you would act so stupidly!" shouted Ralph.

Peggy didn't bother to answer. She buried her head on her arms and cried softly.

Ralph was frightened. "Peggy," he called gently.

Peggy didn't answer.

"Peggy," he called again, "I didn't intend to be mean. But, don't you see—now we have no money left and can't make another call?"

Peggy sat up, took off her cap, and ran her fingers through her hair. It only made her look more bedraggled than ever.

"But I'm so tired," she said, "and I'm quite dizzy from hunger."

"I'll walk to Plips alone to look for Pastor Krog," said Ralph with determination. "You two stay here and rest."

"No, no, please don't," said Peggy quickly. "Then you won't come back and that would be the end."

"All right," said Ralph and got up. "Pull yourself together then. It can't be so far to Plips anymore. A quarter of a mile at the most."

Peggy put her cap back on and smiled again. "All right, I'm coming," she said.

Jim was lying on his stomach and didn't move. He had fallen asleep.

11

Even Bacon and Eggs

"Jim!" urged Ralph. "We have to move on!"

"Can't we wait until he wakes up by himself?" asked Peggy. She loved her brother. The only time she couldn't stand him was when he was naughty.

"No," said Ralph, "then we might fall asleep ourselves. That won't do." He was about to shake Jim when there was a drone from above and three helicopters emerged from the clouds. They were bigger than the helicopters carrying the newspaper reporters. The fuselage was painted blue and white with a golden crown set in a red shield. For a while, they hung motionless above the children. Ralph and Peggy could see men in uniform at the controls. Some of the men looked at them through binoculars.

"We won't harm you! We won't harm you!" shouted Peggy. But the propellers made such a loud noise that she couldn't hear herself above the noise. Neither did the helicopters come any closer. Finally they were swallowed up by the gray clouds sweeping across the sky.

"They took a close look at us," said Ralph. "Did you notice that the men wore uniforms?"

"I hope the Lilliputians won't do anything to us," said Peggy apprehensively.

"What could the Lilliputians possibly do to us?" asked Ralph.

"They shot arrows at Gulliver."

"That was a long time ago. Two hundred and fifty years ago, as Mr. Krumps said. In the meantime, they've kept up with the times."

"Then they might shoot at us with cannons," said Peggy.

"Rubbish!" said Ralph slowly.

"Or they'll throw bombs at us," Peggy insisted. She had a vivid imagination.

Ralph was very disturbed. The thought of cannons, bombs, and the like hadn't even occurred to him.

"We have to reach Pastor Krog as quickly as possible," he said. "Jim has to wake up at once."

When they looked around, Jim was sitting up in the grass, sleepily rubbing his eyes.

"There was a hum," he murmured. "Are we home?"

"No, we're still in Lilliput," said Peggy. "We've got to get to Pastor Krog quickly."

"Lilliput?" Jim said, startled. "I thought that was all a dream."

"You didn't dream that; we are really in Lilliput."

"That's right," said Ralph, nodding at him.

"Where's my gun?" Jim asked suddenly, looking around for it. "I've lost my gun!"

"Mr. Krumps is keeping it for you," said Peggy. "You mustn't run around with a gun in Lilliput; otherwise they might shoot at us with cannons."

Jim looked horrified. "Then I'll knock them all for a loop," he yelled.

"You'll do nothing of the sort," Ralph said sternly. "Now, let's get going."

"But my foot hurts so," complained Jim. He took off his right shoe and showed Peggy his sore foot. There was a blister on his heel.

"Oh, dear, it looks awful!" said Peggy sympathetically.

"That's nothing," said Ralph disdainfully. "When I trekked with my father through the great sand deserts, I often got blisters on my feet. He just laughed at me."

"But it hurts like the dickens," said Jim angrily.

"You're a boy and no longer a baby," Peggy reminded him. "A boy shouldn't whimper."

"How can I help it if I'm a boy," said Jim, sulking. But then he put his shoe back on and got up with a groan.

Drops of rain started to fall, and Ralph urged them to hurry. At the exit of the expressway there was a sign that said in bold letters, "Exit Number 3," and below it, "To Plips ¼ mile."

"Only another quarter of a mile," said Ralph cheerfully. "Just a stone's throw."

"Like fish!" pouted Jim. "I can barely limp." Fretfully, he hobbled behind them.

The road to Plips had three lanes, with two white lines on either side, and there were the same narrow ditches. Gradually, the countryside grew more suburban. Little garden shacks and bungalows alternated with housing developments and, here and there, there were factories surrounded by parking lots. Somewhere the children could hear dogs barking, and every once in a while they could see a few Lilliputians running for cover. Jim insisted that people were looking at them from behind their windows.

"Don't wave," ordered Ralph. "They might think we are threatening them."

As they approached Plips, road signs appeared

on either side of the highway. One read, "Grand Hotel, Plips, One Hundred Rooms with Telephone and Bath." Another one said, "Timko Trucks and Tractors are Superior."

One billboard, bigger than the others, depicted a chef in a kitchen. He was holding a plate of fried eggs and bacon, smiling ecstatically as though he had just won the sweepstakes. This poster read:

AT HOME, ABROAD, WHEREVER YOU GO,
WHEN YOU WANT BACON, ASK FOR KRISPO

"How mean!" said Peggy, and stared wistfully at the picture of eggs and bacon. "I'm so starved, I could eat the whole billboard!"

"If you hold out a little longer, we will soon get something to eat," said Ralph encouragingly. "Perhaps even bacon and eggs."

"And perhaps some hot chocolate?" Jim asked eagerly.

The road ended at a small square. A wide paved avenue began at the other side, with streetcar tracks down the middle. There were cables across the avenue at regular intervals. The cables came up to knee level, and Ralph walked on merely by stepping over them. But, after a few strides, he gave up because it was very exhausting. Peggy and Jim, too, were much too tired to follow him. Ralph kneeled down and tried, Indian-style, to crawl underneath the cables. Pretending to be undaunted, he called: "This is the way to do it!"

"I'm not going to try that," cried Peggy, and sat down in the middle of the pavement.

"Nor will I," echoed Jim, and slumped down beside her. Ralph crawled back to them.

"But you can't just sit here," he said nervously. Ever since Peggy had mentioned the cannons and bombs, he was determined not to leave his friends alone, come what may.

"I'm not going to crawl all the way to Plips," Peggy declared stubbornly.

"Neither am I," repeated Jim, stretching out as though he wanted to sleep again. Helplessly, Ralph looked around. A street at the side of the square led to a housing development. Behind that, it curved in the direction of Plips.

"Get up at once!" Ralph ordered. "We will take this street. I think it will take us to Plips. It's probably just a small detour."

After they had walked through the development, they entered a sprawling wooded park. Its trees were somewhat taller than those at the beach and had a different appearance. In the middle of the woods, the road abruptly came to an end just as if it had been gobbled up.

"This is curtains!" said Peggy, and sat down again. She pushed back her cap, put her arms over her knees, and looked at Ralph reproachfully.

"Curtains nothing," Ralph declared obstinately. Through the trees he could see railway tracks shining, and he called jubilantly: "Hurray! There are railroad tracks!"

Peggy and Jim could not understand why he was so elated.

"What a break!" declared Ralph. "All we have to do is follow the tracks to Plips. A little while ago I noticed that after crossing the river they run directly into Plips."

"Great!" called Jim. He had always wanted to walk on railroad tracks.

"Is that allowed?" asked Peggy anxiously.

"Who's going to stop us?" asked Ralph. "This is an emergency; it's the only way we can proceed." Even he had reached the point where he didn't care.

"But what are we going to do if a train comes?" asked Jim.

"We'll see it from quite a distance," said Ralph. "At least there is some advantage in our being giants."

There were several tracks on the roadbed, and

each could have a pair to himself. In the beginning, they made good progress, but after a while the narrow, hard tracks began to hurt their feet so badly that they could not take another step. Now they were sorry that they wore soft sneakers. To walk between the tracks was even worse because of the small, pointed gravel stones that pricked them like glass splinters.

Peggy threw herself down on the edge of the forest and sobbed. "I can't go on."

Jim sat on a fallen tree trunk and again took off his shoes. Frowning, he stared at the soles of his feet. They had red bruise marks.

"My feet are completely ruined," he moaned.

Ralph too was exhausted. He took off his helmet and fanned the air. Despite the overcast sky, it was very sultry. Somewhere in the distance, a locomotive blew its whistle. At first he paid no attention to it. Then quickly he stepped on the lower branch of a tree to look for the train.

"There's a train coming and it's going to Plips!" he yelled.

Reluctantly, Peggy sat up. "But we aren't on the tracks now," she said.

Ralph jumped down from the tree. "You know what?" he called excitedly.

"No, what?" asked Peggy and Jim.

"We'll stop the train and ask the conductor to take us along."

Peggy and Jim were uncertain.

"We'll never fit inside those small cars," said Peggy.

"Not inside, but on top," explained Ralph gleefully.

Peggy's eyelids fluttered, "You mean on top of the roofs?"

"Yes, of course," said Ralph blissfully. "Couldn't be simpler. There's no other way. We have to get to Plips no matter what."

"Will the cars hold up under our weight?" asked Jim.

"Sure," said Ralph. "They look very sturdy. Besides, they're not that small."

"Why, of course!" said Peggy happily. "Aunt Cornelia told me that her brother-in-law was fabulously rich. He has a model railroad on his farm. When people come to visit him, he always takes them around in it. They too sit on the roofs."

"Boy," cried Jim, "that's great!"

"I saw a picture in a magazine of such a model railway," said Ralph, "with people sitting on top of it. Grownups at that. The cars were no bigger than those we've just seen."

"Do you think that the conductor will let us on?" asked Peggy.

"He'll have to," said Ralph, determined. "We'll beg him. We'll tell him that we'll starve to death if he doesn't. I'm sure he'll understand."

"Oh, dear," said Peggy. "But the railway in Lilliput is a real railway. Surely we'll have to buy tickets and we don't have any money."

"Hmm," said Ralph, out of sorts. Again he had forgotten about having to pay.

"Perhaps we can owe them," suggested Jim. He was disappointed. He would have loved to go on the small railway.

Ralph, feeling dejected, shook his head. "One can't owe a railway anything," he said.

In the meantime, the train was coming nearer, and the children could already hear the pounding of the wheels. A trail of smoke was rising above the

treetops. Presently, an old-fashioned steam locomotive appeared around the bend, followed by a long string of cars.

"Hurray!" screamed Ralph. "It's a freight train. It won't cost anything!"

The children got onto the tracks and waved. The miniature train rapidly came toward them, as though the engineer hadn't seen them at all. The children were just going to jump out of the way when the brakes screeched. With a shower of sparks the locomotive jolted to a stop. No sooner had the train come to a standstill than the engineer leaped out of the right side of the engine cab and the fireman out of the left side. One ran off to the forest at the right, the other to the forest at the left. The brakeman jumped from the last car, far in the rear, and also disappeared like lightning. All this happened before the children could even say "boo."

"Mr. Engineer! Mr. Engineer!" cried Peggy. "Please, oh please, come back!"

But they might just as well have pleaded with a mouse. The engineer took off through the forest as though he were chased by a dinosaur.

12

Toot! Toot! Toot!

"An engineer shouldn't be so frightened," exclaimed Peggy, completely disgusted.

"I wouldn't have expected that," murmured Ralph sadly.

"Maybe he never saw a giant before," commented Jim.

"I could try to call him once more," suggested Peggy.

"Hopeless," said Ralph. "Nothing could stop him."

"Shall I catch him?" asked Jim, ready to take off in pursuit.

"Shut up!" Ralph stormed. "As though Lilliputians were a lot of mice!"

The children could not think of anything to say. Above them there was again a roar as though twenty helicopters were flying around. Probably they were looking for the children but could not find them because the clouds were hanging low. Nervously, Ralph squinted at the sky. Then he studied the train that was standing on the middle track. The engine was hissing and puffing steam as though it was impatient to move on. Filled with curiosity, Jim walked over to it and bent down to look into the engine cab. The back of the cab was open, so that Jim was able to look closely at the many levers, valves, and gauges. But, with Ralph near him, he did not dare touch them.

"It's a beauty!" he called. "I once had a steam engine just like this."

"Kids!" Ralph suddenly called excitedly. "Hold everything!"

"What?" asked Peggy and Jim eagerly.

"We'll run the train ourselves!"

"W . . . what?" Peggy stammered.

Jim bounced up with excitement. "Hurray! I'll run it!"

"No, I will," said Ralph sternly. "We'll have to be very careful so that nothing happens. This is a ticklish job. But it isn't so far to Plips any more. And we can't just perish here miserably, so close to our goal. We have to take a chance in order to win."

"But do you know how to drive a locomotive?" asked Peggy.

"No," admitted Ralph, "but this one shouldn't be too difficult. After all, it's so tiny it's almost like a toy. We'll just have to try; otherwise we're licked."

Peggy was forced to agree.

"As a matter of fact, I've already figured out how we can do it." Again he examined the train carefully. Behind the tender there was a long string of freight cars. Each was about twelve inches high and twenty inches long. The roofs were almost as wide as the width of a step.

"Now listen carefully. I'll lie behind the tender, on the first three cars, so that I can reach the levers of the engine. You'll sit on the roofs—Jim right behind me and then you, Peggy. You'll have to keep an eye on him so that he won't play any foolish tricks."

"I won't play any tricks," protested Jim, tense with eagerness.

"Don't you dare! I won't be able to watch out for you. I'll have to keep my eyes glued to the tracks to see whether all is clear ahead."

"What are we going to do if there is a tunnel or an overhead bridge?" Peggy asked nervously.

"There are no more tunnels," said Ralph, "because there are no hills around. And if we get to a bridge, we'll stop, get off, pull the train under it, and then get on at the other side."

"But there might be a train coming in the other direction," Peggy suggested. She still was not convinced.

"Jumping kangaroo!" exclaimed Ralph, irritably. "Do you just want to sit here until they throw bombs on your head?" Nervously, he looked up at the sky. True, the helicopters had disappeared, but he didn't trust the peace.

"No!" Peggy cried, horrified.

"Okay, then. The train coming from the other direction will be on the other tracks. Besides, I'll see it soon enough. Let's go." He lay down on the first three cars, which were almost exactly his length. Looking over the locomotive, he could see the tracks ahead but not the levers inside the cab because the coal was piled up in front of his nose. He hugged the coal car with his arms and reached inside the cab of the engine. He could feel the levers with his fingers.

"How do you let the steam in, Jim?" he called.

Peggy and Jim were sitting behind him on the car roofs.

"It's a very long lever. Shove it to the right," called Jim, proud to show his knowledge. "But first you have to release the brakes."

"You don't say," answered Ralph irritably. He had found the big lever. "But where's the brake?"

"It should be a small lever or a small valve on the right or left side."

"Holy mackerel!" groaned Ralph. "There are millions of valves and levers!" He felt around and turned a few valves.

Suddenly, a sigh ran through the whole length of the train, as though somebody was letting out his breath. Jim yelled, "Good, those were the air brakes! Now push the big lever to the right."

Ralph shoved the lever as far as it would go and, with a jerk and a jolt, the train got into motion. Jim tumbled backwards on top of Peggy and both fell off the roofs onto the tracks.

"Help!" cried Peggy, but the train moved on without them.

"Ralph! Ralph!" shouted Jim.

Ralph turned around. "What on earth do you think you're doing?" he called, startled. "Why aren't you sitting on the roofs?"

"We fell off," called Peggy. "You started with such a jerk."

"Why don't you stop?" shouted Jim. The train kept on moving.

"I don't know how," said Ralph. "I've forgotten where the brake is."

Peggy and Jim ran after him. "Push back the

big lever," Jim called furiously. The sharp stones were cutting into his thin soles.

Ralph pulled back the lever and the train slowed down. "Jump on!"

Peggy and Jim caught up with him and jumped on the roofs. "Phew!" groaned Peggy. "You'd better be more careful."

"Hold onto the sides. I might have to put on the brakes suddenly."

"Please don't," Peggy implored him.

"How can you brake when you don't know where the brake lever is?" called Jim.

"I have an idea," said Ralph. "I'll simply brake with my feet." He showed them what he meant by letting his legs dangle and braking with his feet as if he were on a sled. The train actually slowed down a bit.

"That's fine," said Peggy approvingly.

Once more, Ralph pushed the big lever to the right and they picked up speed.

"This is wonderful," Peggy remarked. Her hair whipped around her ears and she pushed her cap down on her head.

Jim was all aglow. "Boy, this is great!" he called. The telegraph poles went whizzing by, the wheels were going "click, click, click," and the locomotive puffed busily. A thin streak of smoke from the locomotive stack hit their faces, but that couldn't be helped and it didn't bother them.

Peggy was very happy in spite of being tired and hungry. She got a great thrill out of the trip on the little railway. It made her think of a song that her Grandmother Gertrude had always sung. Gaily she began to hum:

> I've been working on the railroad
> All the livelong day.

Then the sirens sounded again, and she stopped her singing.

"The sirens are wailing again," she said nervously.

"Let them," Ralph answered defiantly.

After leaving the forest, the tracks led up an incline, which went higher and higher until they could look down upon a maze of streets, squares, and housetops. Apparently this was a suburb of Plips. The streets were deserted. The pavements, still wet from a recent downpour, glistened. The familiar canals were everywhere, and now they were full of water.

"Kids," said Ralph, above the sound of the sirens, "at last I know what the canals are for."

"For what?" called Peggy.

"So that the rainwater will run off quickly. Clear as mud. Otherwise, the Lilliputians could not get through the puddles."

"Of course," called Peggy. "If they fell into a puddle they would drown. They're so tiny."

The roadbed started to drop, and presently they were rolling level with the ground. To the right and the left were wire fences and, where the streets crossed the tracks there were gates with guard-

houses. All the gates had been lowered. The train
seemed to be on schedule. Behind the gates waited
long columns of cars, full of Lilliputians and piled
high with baggage. Apparently they were refugees
on their way to the expressway. Ralph gave the
engine more steam, and they fairly whizzed past.
Peggy would have loved to wave to the people, but
she remembered that Ralph had forbidden her.

"Lucky for us the gates have been lowered!"
Ralph called cheerfully.

"Lucky for the Lilliputians, I'd say!" said Jim with a grin.

They banked into a curve, and when they had straightened out, a railroad station zoomed toward them. It was a suburban station with two open platforms on each side of the tracks.

Ralph discovered to his horror that the platforms were crowded with people, trunks, bundles, and crates. They were refugees waiting for a passenger train. The station loomed nearer and nearer, and Ralph yelled, "Jim! Jim! Where is the steam whistle? We have to warn these people."

"It's a lever below the roof of the cab," yelled Jim. "Pull it!"

Feverishly, Ralph pulled a number of levers but to no avail. "Jim, give a toot!" he yelled desperately.

"How can I?" shouted Jim. "My arm won't reach that far."

"I mean toot with your mouth," roared Ralph impatiently.

"Toot! Toot! Toot!" Jim yelled as they whisked past the platform. The people screamed and ran for cover. Most of them tried to squeeze through the exits all at once. Some fled into the waiting rooms. Several men dove headfirst into the newsstands, and all the newspapers scattered on the platform. Others ducked behind the trunks and bundles, and a few simply threw themselves flat on the ground and pretended to be dead. Only one man remained on his feet. He wore a white visor cap, waved a stick furiously, and blew a shrill whistle without stopping. But the children didn't even hear it. The sirens were still wailing everywhere. "Toot! Toot! Toot!" Jim shouted like mad. His face was crimson red. And Peggy yelled without stopping, "We won't harm you! We won't harm you!"

At last, Ralph got his hands on a bell or something resembling it. It rang, "Bing, bing, bing!" almost deafening him.

"Great kangaroo!" called Ralph, as though he had just escaped from a nightmare. "That was a close shave!"

"My tooting was great," yelled Jim.

"Hurray! There's Plips!" Ralph shouted jubilantly. They were racing toward a railway bridge that spanned the river. On the far shore rose the buildings and towers of Plips.

"Will the bridge hold us?" asked Peggy, frightened.

"It's got to," shouted Ralph, and set his jaw.

Peggy closed her eyes as they thundered across the bridge. Arched iron girders flitted by them, the bridge quivered and rocked under their weight, but they reached the other side safely and continued on a high embankment with many tracks, switches, and signals. Frantically, Ralph kept his eyes glued to the tracks, which flashed by below. They pounded over countless switches, leading them off to the left until they reached the last track where the side of the roadbed dropped steeply to a street.

"Look out!" Ralph heard Jim shout. He looked up and saw, to his horror, that they were racing toward a railway terminal. It had a vaulted roof with many small windows in the front. Across it was written, "Plips Terminal." A girder supported by pillars ran the full width of the entrance. Ralph realized that they could never pass under it. "Hold on tight!" he yelled.

"Put on the brakes," squeaked Peggy.

"I can't," yelled Ralph.

"Why don't you use your feet?" shouted Jim.

"How can I?" cried Ralph. On the left ran a wire fence, and on the right, standing on a side track, was an empty passenger train, so that Ralph could not drop his legs to brake with his feet. He pushed the big lever to the left, but it was too late and the station was already almost above them. In a flash, Ralph lowered his head and bumped the girder like a ram. His helmet was pushed over his ears, thick streams of clouds hissed around him, but the train stopped. Ralph stayed on until he found the brake again. He was determined not to allow the train to roll into the station out of control. Only when the brakes creaked the whole length of the train did he gingerly get up to make sure that the train would not move. Then he tore off his helmet and cried cheerfully, "We've done it!" Proudly, he turned around, but Peggy and Jim had disappeared.

"Peggy, Jim!" he called, beside himself. "Where are you?"

"Here," sounded a pitiful squeak. Peggy was lying in some shrubs at the foot of the steep embankment. Jim lay close by. Ralph leaped down the embankment.

"Are you hurt?" he asked, frightened.

"No," said Peggy and sat up. "It just pricks." She had fallen into a bed full of small rose vines.

Jim sat bolt upright. "Boy!" he said. "Some trip, that!" Then he limped after his helmet, which had rolled into the middle of the street. Ralph was grateful that nothing had happened to them.

"How did you manage to land here?" he asked in amazement.

"When you rammed the station with your head, we got thrown over the fence and rolled down the embankment," said Peggy, smiling weakly. Ralph helped her up and brushed her off. She was covered with tiny rose leaves.

"I had to brake somehow," he said, apologizing.

"Of course," said Peggy, with a sigh of resignation. "It just all happened a bit suddenly."

"Lucky that I wore my helmet," said Ralph. "Otherwise, I would have had a honey of a bump. But the main thing is that we finally arrived in Plips. Now all we've got to do is to find Pastor Krog."

He looked around eagerly. They had landed on a wide boulevard. Opposite the embankment stood modern apartment houses with balconies. Ralph could easily have peeked into the sixth floor. Peggy reached to the fifth, Jim only to the fourth. The boulevard led directly into Plips, and the children could see a large square surrounded by beautiful buildings. In the middle of the square was a lawn, and back of it stood a monument and a church with three towers.

"That could be the Kalinda Church," suggested Ralph hopefully. The sirens had stopped.

The children walked toward the square. By now, Jim was limping so badly that Peggy and Ralph had to help him along. They had almost reached the square when a car with blue and white stripes shot out of a side street, raced toward them, and came to a stop right at their feet. On the front and on the back of it it said "Police." A man wearing a blue and white uniform and a white steel helmet jumped out and planted himself in front of them, raising a white stick.

"Halt! Put up your hands and don't move."

Frightened, the children raised their arms.

13

As Big as a Church Tower

The policeman looked courageous and very determined. Obviously, he was in no joking mood.

Sheepishly, Ralph squinted at the church in the background. The clock read exactly twelve, and suddenly the bells began to chime. Perhaps Pastor Krog was in the church, and here they were only a few paces away from their destination but unable to reach it because the policeman would not let them pass.

"What a tough break!" murmured Ralph.

"Do you want me to blow him down?" growled Jim.

"Be quiet! Don't you see? He's a policeman."

"But he's just a midget."

"That's neither here nor there. A policeman is a policeman whether he is a midget or a giant. We've got to do what he tells us."

Peggy could hardly keep her arms up. "Why

should we hold our arms up, officer?" she asked timidly. She had never had anything to do with the police before except that once she had asked a policeman in Sydney for directions. He had been very polite.

"You speak English?" asked the policeman, surprised.

"Oh, yes," said Peggy pleasantly. "How else could we have understood you?"

"That's right," murmured the policeman, rattled. "What are those helmets you are wearing?" he asked Ralph and Jim sternly.

"Those are tropical helmets," replied Ralph quickly. "They protect us from the sun."

The policeman looked up at the sky and saw nothing but clouds. "Is that so?" he snarled, full of suspicion. "Are you armed?"

"No, upon our word of honor," protested Ralph.

"We don't need any arms," grunted Jim. "If I wanted to, I would simply put you in my pocket."

Luckily, the policeman did not hear him because, just at that moment, all the other church bells of Plips started to ring.

"You can drop your arms," he called, "but stay where you are and don't move."

Relieved, the children put down their arms. Jim put his hands in his pants pockets.

"You there, take your hands out of your pockets at once!" cried the policeman, and threateningly pointed his tiny white stick at him. Quickly, Jim took his hands out of his pockets.

"Please don't shoot!" Peggy cried in terror. "We are not real giants, we are just children. We don't want to harm anyone."

"By Gulliver!" cried the policeman, dumbfounded. "You are children?"

"Yes," said Peggy gently. "I am a girl." She took off her cap, bent her head, and allowed her long hair to drop into her face.

"A girl!" cried the policeman, and stared at her, aghast. Peggy was embarrassed.

"My hair looks a mess," she said apologetically and tried to smooth it out. "I left my comb at home."

"A girl!" repeated the policeman, still very much surprised. Then he ran toward his car, pulled out a microphone, and excitedly yelled into it: "Calling headquarters, calling headquarters. Prowl car 22, Sergeant Thompson speaking."

"Here, Lieutenant Boll, come in, Sergeant," the loudspeaker on the dashboard squawked. The church bells had stopped ringing and the children could understand every word clearly.

"Lieutenant, I have arrested the giants," reported the sergeant breathlessly.

"Thunder and lightning!" squawked the loud-speaker. "All by yourself, Sergeant?"

"That's right, Lieutenant. The giants are completely harmless. They are children. Two boys and one girl."

"What? How? Do I read you right? Did you say a girl?"

"That's right, Lieutenant, a little girl."

"A little girl? You've arrested two giants and a little girl?"

"No, Lieutenant, three giants. The girl is a giant little girl—I mean, the girl is a little giant girl." The sergeant was a bit confused. Probably he was very excited. "A very pretty girl at that, Lieutenant."

Ralph and Jim looked at Peggy and grinned. Peggy beamed and stuck out her tongue at them.

"A giant girl? By Gulliver!" squawked the lieutenant through the loudspeaker. "How big is that girl?"

"As big as our church tower. She's got hands like ironing boards and feet like coal barges."

Bewildered, Peggy looked at her hands and feet. Jim snickered shamelessly.

"Are you sure you're right, Sergeant?" the lieutenant began again. "Is it really a girl?" He still could not believe it.

"She says herself that she's a girl," said the

sergeant. "She wears pants but looks like a girl. She also has beautiful long hair."

Peggy started to beam all over again.

"What am I going to do with the giant children, Lieutenant? Request your instructions."

"Where are you, anyway?"

"Near the station."

"Stay where you are. Wait until I get there. Meanwhile, I'm sending you reinforcements. First, I have to send a flash to all departments and the press. Congratulations, Sergeant. I'll put in for your promotion."

"Thanks, Lieutenant," said the sergeant. Now he too was beaming. He had hardly hung up when six or eight motorcycles, sirens howling, came racing toward them as though they wanted to break all speed records. With brakes screeching, they came to a stop in front of the children. The motorcycle policemen wore white uniforms and steel helmets just like the sergeant. They stared at the children in utter amazement. At last, one of them jumped off, ran over to the sergeant, and called: "Heartiest congratulations, Sergeant. You did a great job."

"Nothing to it," the sergeant replied casually. "I was watching those giants tumble down the side of the railway embankment and said to myself, 'Now or never.' So, I just arrested them. They wanted to march into the city. And since the city has not been evacuated, it was up to me to stop them at all costs."

The other policemen surrounded the sergeant, too, and congratulated him. They talked and laughed excitedly, but the children could not understand anything because it was all drowned out in the sudden roar of hundreds of radios from the houses nearby. An announcer shouted: "Attention! Attention! This is an official bulletin! The giants have been arrested in Plips. They are completely harmless. They are children. Two boys and one girl. The state of emergency has been lifted."

The broadcast had scarcely finished when windows were thrown open and Lilliputians peered out from everywhere. Many came running out and crowded the sidewalks near where the children were standing in the middle of the street. Others poured in from the side streets, and the air was filled with the murmur of excited voices.

"Just look at those giants! My, how eerie! And just look at that girl. A giant girl!" they repeated over and over.

With mixed feelings, the children looked down upon an ocean of heads. Peggy smiled pleasantly. Ralph squinted with embarrassment. Jim grinned and rolled his eyes a bit. He was proud that so many people were afraid of him.

All the Lilliputians were well dressed. The men wore dapper suits, and the women were in colorful dresses. Even the children looked nicely turned out. The boys wore short pants and jackets and the girls dresses or skirts and blouses.

The crowd increased to an alarming extent, and the sergeant ordered the policemen to block off the street.

The policemen linked arms and kept shouting: "Get back! Get back, folks! Don't come into the street. Don't push. Stay off the street."

The sergeant pulled out a notebook. "Now I have to take down some personal data about you," he said with an air of authority. "What's your name?" he asked Peggy.

"Peggy Warner," said Peggy.

"How old?"

"I'm eleven years old," said Peggy, "but Mommy always says I'm very tall for my age."

The throng roared with laughter, but it was not unfriendly.

"And you?" the sergeant asked Jim. "What's your name?"

"Jim," said Jim.

"He's my brother," said Peggy, "and he's nine."

"Nine?" the throng murmured in complete disbelief.

The sergeant turned to Ralph. "Name, please."

"Ralph Henderson," murmured Ralph, clearing his throat, "and I'm thirteen."

"How did you get to Lilliput?" asked the sergeant.

"Well, it was like this," Peggy began.

A hush fell over the crowd and everyone listened intently, but Peggy was not in the least embarrassed. After all, the people were only as big as little dolls.

"At first, I didn't want to come," she continued cheerfully, "but Jim kept nagging me and Ralph didn't seem to object, although our parents had strictly forbidden us to row out to sea. They won't even let us go swimming in the ocean on account of the many sharks. As a matter of fact, Jim fell into the water, and if Ralph hadn't grabbed him by his hair, he might have been bitten by a shark."

"Hm," the sergeant interrupted her. "And how did you get to Lilliput?"

"In a rubber raft," interrupted Ralph quickly. Peggy looked at him, a bit hurt. "We couldn't buck the wind. All the while it was blowing out of the east. We drifted for a whole day and half a night."

"It was terrible," said Peggy. "It was awfully rough and I felt sick."

The Lilliputians laughed again good-naturedly.

"Why did you come to Plips?" asked the sergeant. "We thought that you would take the expressway and march on Mildendo, our capital."

"We wanted to go to the Kalinda Church," said Ralph.

The sergeant was dumbfounded. "You know that there is a Kalinda Church in Plips?" he cried.

"We would like to speak to Pastor Krog," said Ralph.

"You even know Pastor Krog?" cried the sergeant, even more dumbfounded.

"We don't know him," said Peggy, "but Mr. Krumps knows him very well. He told us that we should turn to Pastor Krog."

"Krumps? Do you mean Hank Krumps who has the big farm near the expressway?"

"Yes," said Peggy. "He has white hair, smokes a pipe, and is very sunburned."

"But didn't Hank Krumps pull out before you came?"

"Oh, no," said Peggy, "he had to bring in his hay. He was very kind. He even loaned us a dimeling so that we could call Pastor Krog, but the operator wouldn't connect us because it wasn't urgent. That's why we came ourselves. It wasn't so easy at that," she added with a sigh.

"Excuse me," said Ralph, "but is that the Kalinda Church over there on the square?"

"No, that's the Plips Cathedral. The Kalinda Church is in the center of the town in the Mully Ully Gue Street. Pastor Krog is not in Plips right now. He's in Tottenham on the west coast."

14

Raindrops Can Kill

Pastor Krog not here! The children were so disappointed they did not know what to say.

"What did you want from Pastor Krog?" asked the sergeant finally.

"Is it very far to Tottenham?" croaked Ralph.

"Very," said the sergeant. "Forty miles. Twelve hours with the fastest train."

"But that's awful," cried Peggy almost in tears. "Mr. Krumps assured us that Pastor Krog would help us. The fact is that we're very hungry," she added a little shyly. "Since yesterday we've had nothing to eat and only a little water from the brook to drink."

"Dear, dear, listen, listen, the giant children are hungry." The Lilliputians were very touched.

"Great guns!" cried the sergeant.

Peggy winced.

"Nothing to eat?" the sergeant went on, genuinely concerned. "Well, we'd better feed you first. What sort of things do you eat?"

"Why, everything," said Peggy, encouraged. "Meat, vegetables, fish, butter, and bread. We'd also eat hot sausages. At home, I always drink a lot of milk," she admitted.

"I'd like some hot chocolate," said Jim.

"Don't be so greedy!" Peggy hissed at him. "We have to eat what we get. After all, we are their guests."

Once more, the sergeant ran over to his car and called into the microphone: "Calling headquarters, calling headquarters."

"What's the trouble?" the loudspeaker squawked nervously. "Don't tell me the giant children got away from you, Sergeant."

"No, Lieutenant, they are behaving beautifully. Except that they are completely famished. Would you have anything for them to eat?"

"To eat? By Gulliver! What do these giant children eat?"

"Everything, Lieutenant. Meat, vegetables, fish, butter, and bread. They would also eat hot sausages. The girl drinks a lot of milk at home."

"Milk? The giant girl wants milk? How much milk do you suppose we would need?"

The sergeant examined Peggy to make an estimate. "Well, at least a quart anyway, Lieutenant."

"A quart!" the Lilliputians shouted, completely astounded.

"A quart!" the lieutenant also cried. "Why, that's almost a whole tank car full. I'll call the Hellinger Dairy right away."

"And the boy would like to have some hot chocolate, Lieutenant," reported the Sergeant dutifully.

"Hot chocolate? Are you out of your mind? Where do you want me to get that much chocolate so quickly? After all, I can't be expected to make three bathtubs full of it."

"We really don't need any hot chocolate," Ralph called hastily.

Jim glowered at him furiously.

"Cancel the hot chocolate, Lieutenant," said the sergeant, much relieved. "But, with your permission, let the milk order stand." He smiled and winked at Peggy knowingly.

Peggy smiled gratefully.

"The milk, of course," said the lieutenant. "Milk is very good for children. I will refer the other matter to the Refugee Center. But they had better not count on hot sausage. All the Green Cross nurses have been ordered to Wiggywack. They took all the sausage with them."

"We don't need any sausages either," called Ralph again.

When he had accompanied his father through the desert, he had often gone for days on end on only a small food ration.

The sergeant hung up and gave him a friendly nod. Meanwhile, the crowd on the sidewalks had grown huge. Many had climbed up the railway embankment to get a better view. Alarmed, the sergeant looked around. "Come with me," he suddenly called to the children.

"Are you going to lock us up now?" asked Peggy nervously.

"Heavens no!" said the sergeant. "You haven't committed any crime. As long as you behave, you won't be locked up. I'm taking you to Gulliver Square because you will be safer there." He went ahead, but the children hesitated to move.

"Why aren't you following me?" called the sergeant. Once more he had become suspicious.

"Your legs are so short," Peggy said reluctantly. "Ours are so long that we just can't take tiny steps."

Startled, the sergeant looked at his legs; then he looked at the children's. "By Gulliver," he murmured. He took off his helmet and mopped his brow. "Your legs are really gigantic. But wait, I'll get into the car and drive ahead of you, then you can surely follow me. How about it?"

"Oh, yes," said Peggy, "that should work all right."

"Have you got a gun?" asked Jim.

"In Lilliput, the police are unarmed," said the sergeant, and got into his car.

"What kind of a car is this?" said Jim.

"It's a Timko," said the sergeant.

"Are the Timkos the only kind they've got in Lilliput?" asked Jim.

"No," said the sergeant. "We also have Nostas and Winnemanns, but Timkos are superior."

He blew his siren and started up. The police jumped on their motorcycles and rode behind the children. The Lilliputians wanted to follow them, but soon they fell behind.

Jim was still limping badly, but he would not allow Ralph or Peggy to help him now because he was afraid that the Lilliputians might laugh at him. The sergeant stuck his head out of the window and called to Peggy.

"Why is your brother limping?" He had noticed it in his rearview mirror.

"He's got a blister on his heel," called Peggy, "but Ralph says it isn't so bad."

"I'll have a doctor look at him tomorrow," called the sergeant, and pulled his head back inside.

"Ralph can go and fly a kite," murmured Jim. He was still annoyed because he was not going to have hot chocolate.

Gulliver Square was very large, almost as large as the tennis court at home on which they had played only the day before not suspecting what was in store for them. Wide boulevards and shopping streets radiated from the square. Around it stood elegant houses and modern office buildings. Some were built of marble while others had the appearance of Greek temples, with columns in the front and stone figures decorating the cornices. Some of the office buildings were built entirely of glass and aluminum. "Timko" was inscribed on one of them and "Liliko" on another. Flagpoles were mounted on the top of many buildings, and blue-and-white-striped flags were fluttering in the wind. Despite the gray sky, they looked pretty and colorful because they all had a golden crown in a red field, exactly as on the three helicopters the children had seen earlier. In the middle of the square was a large park. On the right, they noticed the terminal station. It sat fairly high at the end of the railway embankment, and two or three dozen wide steps led to the main entrance.

Diagonally across was the Grand Hotel. Next to it stood the town hall. Then came the main post office, museum, several office buildings, and, with a square of its own, the cathedral and its three proud spires, which were almost twice the size of the children. On the other side of Gulliver Square stood a particularly tall building. On the ground floor, it had many shop windows, and mounted on the roof was an iron scaffold carrying a neon sign. "Mintz, the Department Store for Everything and Everybody" was its message. In one corner, where two avenues met in a wide angle, stood a bronze statue. It showed a man who was as tall as the children's own fathers. His clothes were old-fashioned—he wore knee breeches, buckled shoes, and a three-cornered hat. The figure of a Lilliputian, also in old-fashioned dress and pointing his finger at the giant as though in reproach, stood in the palm of his hand. The giant smiled amiably.

The monument made such a great impression on Peggy that she asked a motorcycle policeman who was riding near her left foot: "Excuse me, Mr. Policeman, but what is that lovely statue over there?"

"That's Gulliver in life size," the policeman called up to her. "Don't you know him? He too came from the land of giants."

"I know who Gulliver is," said Peggy, "but I

never met him because he has been dead a long time. And who's the cute little man in his hand?"

"He was the then reigning Emperor, Mully Ully Gue," called the policeman. "He reigned from 1657 to 1746. He is an ancestor of Her Majesty, our beloved Queen Alice."

"Oh," said Peggy respectfully. "Is the queen very old?"

"No, she's still very young," said the policeman.

"We, too, have a queen," said Peggy proudly.

"You don't say," the policeman said in amazement. "She's probably very tall."

"Not at all," said Peggy, a bit offended. "She's no taller than Ralph."

"Jeepers," called the policeman, "she must have a palace as big as a skyscraper."

They crossed the street and headed for the lawn. Ralph noticed again the deep, narrow ditches sunk into the pavement. But, instead of being open, the ditches here were covered with a fine-meshed wire net. This was probably to prevent the Lilliputian children from falling into them.

"Mr. Policeman," Ralph called, "incidentally, what are all those ditches for?" Although he had an idea, he wanted to know exactly.

"They are drain ditches for the rain," the policeman explained willingly.

Ralph was pleased that he had guessed correctly.

"In the old days, when they didn't have these canals," the policeman continued, "every little downpour caused a catastrophe. But, even today they are not without danger. Big raindrops are liable to kill a person. During a cloudburst, the entire traffic is stopped because of the rain lakes."

"Don't the Lilliputians have umbrellas?" Peggy wanted to know.

"They are no good during a cloudburst. That is the reason why any Lilliputian may run into the nearest house when it rains. That is permitted by law."

"We should have that kind of law too," said Peggy approvingly.

They had reached the park and the sergeant called over to them: "Sit down on the lawn over

there. As a matter of fact, it is strictly prohibited, but today we'll close both eyes to enforcing the law!" He grinned over his own joke.

"Many thanks," said Peggy with a sigh of relief. "We're really awfully tired. We've been on our feet since early this morning."

"But we also had a ride on the train," murmured Jim.

The children sat down on the grass, and the sergeant ordered the policemen to rope it off. In the meantime, a vast throng of people had poured into Gulliver Square, and everybody was eyeing the children in amazement. Fathers lifted their young on their shoulders so that they too could see. Young men and boys shinnied up lampposts, and some even climbed on the base of the monument. People were looking out of every window and they crowded balconies and roofs. Many looked down at the giant children through opera glasses or binoculars. The people sitting on the station steps were particularly fortunate. They sat there like spectators in a stadium and didn't have to crane their necks. There was the hum of excited voices, just as at a big football match. Every once in a while, the children could make out a few broken sentences or exclamations. The people seemed to be most intrigued by Peggy.

"Just look at the girl! Heavens, what hair! Like

a waterfall! She's even a pretty girl. I'd hate to be that tall, must be awful!"

In vain, Peggy tried again to smooth out her hair. Jim yawned loudly.

"I feel like a monkey in a cage," he murmured, and stretched out.

Ralph looked around with curiosity. Even when they were sitting, the children were tall enough to look above all the people into the square.

"There's a post office over there," he whispered excitedly to Peggy. "Perhaps we could send a wire home from there."

"That's wonderful," said Peggy, but suddenly she remembered that it was Sunday. "Oh, dear," she cried, "don't you remember that it's Sunday today and that all the post offices are closed?"

"Nuts!" Ralph said, bitterly disappointed.

15

C as in Chocolate

Sadly, Peggy looked over at the post office. "Ralph," she whispered excitedly a minute later. "The doors are open and I can even see a few people going in."

"That's right," murmured Ralph. "And don't you remember seeing the smoke of factory chimneys on the way here?"

"That's funny," said Peggy. "Mr. Sergeant," she called disarmingly.

The sergeant was just walking toward his car, but he turned around quickly and came back.

"What can I do for you?" he asked, eager to oblige.

"Is the post office open on Sundays too?"

"Of course not on Sundays," said the sergeant.

"But the doors are open," said Ralph.

"Today isn't Sunday; today is Wednesday," said the sergeant.

Peggy and Ralph were astonished. Lilliput must

have a different calendar than Australia. But they were very happy.

"Would you let us run over there to send a telegram?" asked Peggy with a charming smile.

"Oh, my goodness!" said the sergeant, startled. "With all those people? Out of the question. You might endanger hundreds of lives! Where do you want to send the telegram?"

"We want to wire home," said Peggy sadly. "Our poor parents are worrying terribly. We have been gone since yesterday and they don't know where we are."

"By Gulliver, you've got to notify your parents at once. Brax!" he called. "Run over to the post office and get a few telegram blanks."

The policeman disappeared into the crowd, and all the children could see was his white helmet bobbing up and down among all the people. Anxiously, the sergeant and the children looked after him.

"I hope he'll come back alive," said the sergeant jokingly. "What do you want to say in the telegram?"

"We have no money," said Jim.

"Shucks," Peggy cried, and looked at Ralph reproachfully. Hadn't he given them his promise to borrow money? Ralph screwed up all his courage.

"Excuse me very much, Mr. Sergeant," he began

to stammer, "would you have . . . could you . . . could you possibly lend us some money? We are shipwrecked and we have lost all our money."

"We never had any in the first place," said Jim.

"Don't keep butting in all the time," Ralph snapped at him angrily.

The sergeant grinned. "Now, don't get excited," he said. "I'll be glad to lend you a few onzes."

"Onzes?" Peggy asked, confused. "What are onzes?"

"Onzes are Lilliputian money. One onze has ten dimelings and each dimeling has ten bims. When you have a chance, you can return the money to me. How much do you want?"

"At home we don't have onzes," confessed Ralph meekly.

"Neither do we have any bims," added Peggy sadly.

"Well, then, what do you have?" asked the sergeant.

"We have pounds," said Ralph.

"Pounds?" Now it was the sergeant's turn to be confused. "But that is a weight."

"The Australian money is pounds," Peggy explained to him eagerly. "One pound has twenty shillings, and one shilling has twelve pence. We also have sixpence and tuppence and ha'pennies and crowns and half crowns."

"That sounds mighty complicated," said the sergeant, scratching the back of his head. "I wouldn't know what to do with pounds here. Nobody knows them in Lilliput."

"That's very sad," said Peggy.

"Well, don't worry," said the sergeant generously. "I will advance you the few onzes. The Police Treasury will refund them to me. Ah, here is Brax. He made it."

His helmet all askew and with perspiration dripping down his face, Brax appeared and held the telegram blank up to Peggy. Peggy took it between her fingertips and looked at it helplessly. The paper was not even the size of her thumbnail.

"How tiny it is!" she exclaimed.

"We'll manage somehow," said Ralph. "Have you got a pencil?"

Peggy searched in her bag and finally produced the stump of a pencil. Unfortunately, the lead in it was much too thick for the form.

"How can I write with it?" she cried.

"I have a ball pen," said the sergeant, and handed something up to her that looked no bigger than a pine needle.

"I can't write with this either," Peggy declared. "I can't even get hold of it."

"Throw down the telegram form and I'll fill it out for you," said the sergeant obligingly.

Peggy let the form drop on the ground, and the sergeant caught it.

"Now, then, what do you want to wire home?"

"What do we want to wire home?" repeated Peggy, and looked at Ralph expectantly.

Ralph took off his helmet and scratched behind his ear.

"Tell Mommy to send me a bandage for my foot," called Jim, and sat bolt upright.

"That would take too many words," said Peggy. "It would cost too many onzes."

"Stingy," said Jim, and lay down again.

"First dictate the address," suggested the sergeant.

"Warner Farm, Long Hill near Homc, Australia," said Ralph. The sergeant wrote it down and repeated, "Warner Farm—Long Hill—near Homc." He looked up and squinted. "Homc? How do you spell that?"

"H—O—M—"

"Hold it, not so fast, young giant. M or N?"

"Let me spell it," cried Peggy eagerly. "I know

how to do it. One has to do it with names. My father always spells that way on the telephone."

"Hom, hom," murmured the sergeant, his ballpoint pen ready for action.

"H as in Hamlet, O as in Othello, M as in Macbeth," Peggy began to spell.

"How, who, what?" asked the sergeant. "What kind of funny names are they?"

"Those are plays by Shakespeare," Peggy explained proudly. "William Shakespeare is our most famous poet. I always listen to his plays on the radio. We don't have television yet because we live in the country, too far away from the big cities. My Aunt Cornelia has three television sets in her house in Sydney. One is even in the kitchen. Besides, one time in school, we read 'Romeo and Juliet,' each taking a part. I was Juliet. My teacher, Miss Lampart, has always said that I was talented."

With that, Peggy began to recite with emotion: "Oh Romeo, Romeo, wherefore art thou Romeo?" At last, she had found a real audience, even though its people were no bigger than trinkets. "Deny thy father and refuse thy name," she continued happily, "or, if thou wilt not, be but sworn my love and I'll no longer be a Capulet." That was all she knew by heart.

Thundering applause rose from Gulliver Square. "Bravo! Bravo!" the Lilliputians yelled with enthusiasm, and, with her face all smiles, Peggy took a bow.

"I can do a trick too," Jim howled, seeking attention. He jumped up and turned a somersault. If they hadn't jumped aside in time, three policemen would have been squashed to death.

The Lilliputians froze in silence. Nobody applauded.

"Quit the horseplay," Ralph shouted at him furiously.

The sergeant just shook his head to show his disapproval. Then he turned to Peggy again.

"Hom, Hom," he murmured impatiently.

"Not Hom," said Peggy, "Homc, c as, c as . . ." She hesitated because she could not think of a play by Shakespeare that began with a c.

"C as in chocolate," interrupted Jim, and gave Ralph a defiant look.

16

No Butter on the Bread!

"C as in chocolate," the sergeant repeated with a sigh. "Well, finally we have the address straight: Warner Farm, Long Hill, near Homc, Australia. In the meanwhile, have you decided what you want to say?"

"We're in Lilliput. Come fetch us. Kisses. Peggy, Jim, Ralph," said Ralph.

The sergeant looked startled and frowned at him. "I'm afraid that won't go through," he said meaningfully.

"Will the kisses make it too expensive?" Peggy asked nervously.

"I don't mind the kisses, but 'come fetch' sounds to me as though it might have a catch to it. I'd better take that up with my boss."

"Why?" protested Peggy and Ralph in unison.

"I'm just a cop," began the sergeant, but he never finished the sentence. From across the square a commanding voice rumbled over the loudspeaker: "Clear the street, folks, clear the street. The street must be cleared."

A column of vehicles appeared out of a side street off Gulliver Square and slowly worked its way through the throng. It was led by three police cars, with blue and white stripes, and a motorcycle escort. Then came a convoy of trucks and a tank truck made of shining metal. Bringing up the rear was a troop of mounted policemen. The horses were no bigger than Chihuahua dogs and looked enchanting. They had long, curly tails and manes, and their brown coats shimmered like silk.

Jim was captivated by the sight of them. He sat up and yelled: "Peggy! Just look at the horses!"

"Move back. Move back, folks," trumpeted the loudspeaker. The mounted police moved up to the head of the column and started to push back the Lilliputians. Now the truck convoy could move closer. The sergeant hastily stuffed the telegram into his pocket.

"We'll talk about it later," he yelled to the children. "My lieutenant is coming."

"Those horses are terrific," cried Jim. "May I pet them?"

"Heavens, no!" said the sergeant. "If you touched them with your giant hands, they would bolt at once."

"I only wanted to touch them very gently," Jim murmured sadly. He was very fond of horses. He and Peggy had two beautiful ponies at home.

The police cars stopped in front of the lawn, and a police officer emerged from the head car, which had a big loudspeaker mounted on the roof. He wore a blue uniform with white epaulets, and the visor of his cap was gold embroidered.

The sergeant ran up to him and saluted. "I'm glad you're here, Lieutenant. We haven't had to cope with such a crowd since Coronation Day. For a moment, I thought we would be trampled down."

"Close off all approaches to the square! Nobody is to be let through anymore! Only officials and members of the press!" barked the lieutenant. The sergeant ran off to relay the orders, and the lieutenant eyed the children.

"By Gulliver!" he murmured. "They are even more frightening than I thought." He put his hand to his visor in salute and nodded at them amiably. "I'm Lieutenant Boll. How are you giant kids?"

"How do you do?" said Peggy and Ralph, a bit absentmindedly. They were still wondering why the sergeant seemed to be bothered by the telegram.

"I'm bringing you some food," said the lieutenant. He was quite stout and looked as though he enjoyed good eating.

"Food!" cried Peggy enthusiastically. "Oh, thank you!" Longingly, she looked at the open trucks, but she could not make out what was in them.

"You're quite welcome," said the lieutenant with a grin. "I'm only sorry you had to wait so long. But I first had to consult Professor Lemmle of the Bureau of Statistics to have him figure out what three giant children might need in calories. It took him a long time to do all the multiplying, dividing, subtracting, and adding. Then he had to square the result, extract roots, only to square the result again, and finally he came up with the quantity of what I had to order. In all the hurry, I could only manage to arrange for cold snacks," he added apologetically. "But tonight you will get some warm food."

"Oh, that doesn't matter. I love cold snacks," said Peggy accommodatingly. "Whenever my Aunt Cornelia has a lot of guests, she serves a cold buffet."

Meanwhile, the trucks had formed a semicircle around the children. Each truck was piled high with food. One was loaded with long bread loaves, another with round balls of cheese, a third with red apples, and the fourth with chocolate bars. The fifth contained something that the children did not recognize, but they were too shy to ask about it. It looked like small, dark gray starfish. The tank truck had painted on it, "Dairy Hellinger—Milk Truck."

"Well, now, help yourselves and eat," the lieutenant invited them. "Or do you mind all the people? If you do, I will have the square cleared."

"Oh, no," said Peggy. "We don't mind the people at all. They are all so kind. Whenever we have a school picnic, we eat with many other children."

Jim immediately reached for the truck with the chocolate bars, but Peggy slapped his hand firmly. "Can't you wait? You're not supposed to start with chocolate. That's the dessert. First you have bread and cheese. Then apples and chocolate. I will hand out the food. Let me have your helmets." Suddenly, she was quite the efficient housewife. For each of them she counted out fifty loaves and fifty balls of cheese.

"That's a very slim portion," Jim complained.

"Plenty for now," declared Peggy. "You can come back for seconds."

Jim took one of the tiny loaves between his thumb and index finger and suspiciously eyed it from all sides. "There's no butter on it," he said sulkily.

Peggy was furious. "Don't be so greedy!"

"What? No butter on the bread?" called Lieutenant Boll. "Thunder and lightning! Holst, why is there no butter on the bread? How come? I expressly ordered butter!"

Patrolman Holst came running up. "I beg your pardon, Lieutenant, there are four hundred and fifty-six loaves. We tried to spread them with butter, but it would have taken us until tonight. We didn't have enough manpower."

"Then you should have called the Fire Department."

"That we did, Lieutenant, but the Fire Department told us that it wasn't their job to spread butter on bread."

"What else are they good for, since there aren't many fires?" growled the lieutenant angrily. "Tomorrow you will get butter on your bread," he called to Jim. "Even if it means spreading butter all night." Probably the lieutenant himself did not like to eat bread without butter.

Jim nodded condescendingly and pushed five cheese balls the size of big marbles into his mouth. Then he stuffed six bread loaves after them. Peggy was eating, too, and the Lilliputians gasped with astonishment. "Look! Just look!" Voices sounded all around them. "Already the girl has devoured ten of the big loaves! And just take a look at the boy! He's pushing those huge cheeses into his mouth as though they were berries!"

Flattered, Jim managed a grin and at once stuffed

another whole handful of cheese balls into his mouth to show what an awe-inspiring giant he was. Peggy felt a little embarrassed and began to eat only one loaf and cheese ball at a time.

Only Ralph wouldn't eat. Instead, he stared into his helmet with a worried expression. "Perhaps we'll have to pay for the food," he whispered to Peggy.

Aghast, Peggy almost choked on a cheese ball. She began to cough and to struggle for air. "P . . . pay?" she croaked, almost suffocating.

Ralph gave her a good slap on the back. "How do we know?" he murmured.

Jim already had finished his share and again held out his helmet to Peggy.

"May I have some more?" he pleaded.

"No," said Peggy, still hoarse.

"Why not?" demanded Jim irritably. "You told me I could have seconds."

"Perhaps we have to pay for it all," Peggy whispered hastily into his ear, "and we don't have any money."

"Jumping kangaroo," Jim answered.

The lieutenant had watched them with curiosity. "Why don't you eat more? The bread comes from Zumke, the finest bakery in Plips. Or don't you like the taste of it?"

"Oh, yes," Peggy assured him.

"And the cheese is the famous Meggendaler, the best in all of Lilliput."

"I love to eat cheese," said Peggy with embarrassment, "but we are shipwrecks."

"So what?" the lieutenant interrupted her, startled. "Can't shipwrecks eat cheese?"

"Oh, yes," Peggy admitted, "shipwrecks can eat anything."

"Pardon me, Mr. Lieutenant." Ralph screwed up his courage. "We have lost our money on the way here and we have no idea whether we are supposed to pay for the food."

"Oh, good Gulliver!" the lieutenant exclaimed. "After all, we can guess that you have no Lilliputian money. You don't have to pay for anything. I've already taken the matter up with the government in Mildendo. They're pleased as punch that you're harmless and haven't caused any destruction in Lilliput. Queen Alice too is very happy about it. You are the guests of honor of the government. Your bed and board are at government expense."

"Boy!" cried Jim, beside himself, and reached for the chocolate bars with both hands. Peggy and Ralph felt relieved and thanked the lieutenant.

"Is there milk in this?" asked Peggy, and longingly eyed the tank car. Although it unmistakably bore the words "Milk Truck," no one had offered them any milk. She was afraid that the Lilliputians might forget about it.

"Thunder and lightning!" exclaimed the lieutenant again. "Sergeant Thompson, milk."

"Good heavens," called the sergeant with concern. "Brax, Miller, Holst! Fetch the pails!"

Brax, Miller, and Holst, with five other policemen, brought up pails to the tank truck and began filling them with milk. Then they formed a human chain to Peggy and handed the pails from hand to hand in the same way as people fight fires in the country. The pails were only the size of tiny goblets, just big enough for one swallow. Without stopping, Peggy emptied thirty-five pails, one after the other, and Ralph and Jim waited impatiently for their turn.

"Let me have a drink too," Jim cried, fidgeting.

At last, Peggy had her fill and Ralph and Jim also drank at least twenty of the small pails of milk. Once more, the Lilliputians were astounded. "Just look, look! They're drinking one pail after the other! Great Gulliver, they have nothing on an elephant!"

Peggy handed out more bread loaves and cheese balls, and after the bread and cheese were gone, she counted out one hundred apples for each of them and one hundred chocolate bars for Ralph and herself. Jim got only fifty as punishment for having

taken some before. After they had finished all the chocolate and apples, they drank some more milk.

"Why don't you try what's on that truck over there?" called the lieutenant, and pointed at the funny, small starfish.

"To eat?" Peggy asked cautiously.

"By Gulliver," the lieutenant cried almost with envy. "That's the greatest delicacy in Lilliput! My children are crazy about it."

Peggy took one of the things resembling a starfish and courageously swallowed it. "It tastes very good," she said with deliberation and rolled her eyes. It tasted like dill pickles and she couldn't stand them.

"I should say so!" said the lieutenant, rubbing his hands. "You can only get it in the best restaurants. They're smoked squid."

"Squid?" stammered Peggy.

Ralph and Jim grinned mischievously.

"You must try some of it too," the lieutenant called to them.

"I don't eat squid," murmured Jim.

"I'm completely full," stammered Ralph.

"Me too," groaned Peggy, and quickly drank another twenty pails of milk.

17

No Telegram

Hardly had the trucks disappeared when a group of men and women were admitted through the police cordon. They had cameras and motion-picture apparatus. Flashlights exploded and cameras began to hum. There was such a commotion around the children that they felt a little dizzy. The women and men were apparently officials or newspaper people; otherwise they would not have been allowed through. One man was particularly distinguished by his dress. He wore a blue silk cape held around his neck by a thick golden chain. His hat was like a flat board, with a silver tassel dangling from it.

"Hello, Lieutenant Boll," he called affably. "I see you've got the giants under control."

"Thank you, my lord," said Lieutenant Boll, "but the credit goes to our Sergeant Thompson, who took them prisoners singlehanded."

"Splendid, Sergeant," said the gentleman. "You

have the gratitude of all of Lilliput. I herewith pro-
mote you to detective third-class."

The sergeant stood at attention and saluted.
"Thank you," he stammered, overcome with emotion.

The gentleman with the cape walked up to Peggy
and stopped in front of her. But, since she was sitting
with her heels on the ground and her toes pointed
upward, her shoe soles towered above him like a
wall so that he had to walk around and approach
her from the side.

"Greetings," he said amiably and bowed.

Peggy and Ralph bowed in reply. Jim yawned.
He was so tired that he forgot to hold his hand in
front of his mouth. The dignified gentleman tactfully
pretended not to notice it.

"My name is Paul Frederick," he said to Peggy.

"I am very pleased to make your acquaintance.
My name is Peggy Warner," she said, more politely
than ever. The gentleman might possibly be a relative of the Queen or a general; in either case one
couldn't be polite enough.

"I greet you in the name of Lilliput and the city
of Plips," continued the gentleman. "I am the Mayor
of Plips."

"Many thanks," said Peggy. "We don't have
mayors because we live on a farm. But there is one

in Home, and my Uncle Max plays Ping-Pong with him."

"Is that so?" said the mayor, looking a bit confused. Obviously, he had never heard of Ping-Pong before. Perhaps it was unknown in Lilliput. "I hope that you had enough to eat and that the food was all right."

"The food was excellent," said Ralph. At last he seemed a bit more at home and no longer so timid. At home the grownups were not nearly as accommodating as the Lilliputians. There was something to being a giant after all.

Peggy was completely at ease in Lilliput. The Lilliputians were charming and treated her almost like a celebrated movie star. "The food was heavenly," she said. "The small bread loaves were crisp and freshly baked, and the cheese balls tasted almost like marzipan. The milk was just like cream."

"I am glad to hear that," said the mayor. He presented all the gentlemen and ladies of his party to the children, but they could not remember a single name in all the confusion.

One gentleman, with a bushy mustache, called up to them, "I'm sincerely sorry that I could not send you any hot sausages. But all the sausages are in Wiggywack. However, I promise you that you will have hot sausages tomorrow morning for breakfast."

"I never eat sausages for breakfast," said Peggy. "But could we perhaps have Krispo bacon?"

The ladies and gentlemen laughed heartily. The gentleman with the mustache seemed very surprised.

"How do you know about Krispo bacon? Do you have it too?"

"Oh, no," said Peggy. "We saw the billboard on the way here. "At home, abroad, wherever you go, when you want bacon, ask for Krispo!" she quoted smugly. She had not forgotten.

The ladies and gentlemen laughed again, and all around the square the people joined them. Some even clapped their hands.

"The bacon looked awfully good," Peggy continued merrily. "My father is very fond of fried bacon for breakfast."

"Of course you can have Krispo bacon for breakfast," said the man with the mustache. "I shall requisition twenty crates at once. My name is Herb Mock, and I'm the Director of the Refugee Center."

"Oh, it's *you!*" Peggy cried excitedly. "Then we know each other." Mr. Mock was speechless. In his entire life he had never known a giant.

"But I spoke to you on the telephone!"

Mr. Mock was even more dumbfounded. "We have spoken to each other on the telephone?"

"Why, yes," said Peggy triumphantly. "I called you from the expressway. You were going to send the police after me if I had the nerve to call you again."

"Great Gulliver! How fantastic! That was you? My dear child, why didn't you tell me that you were a giant?"

"She forgot," Ralph explained.

"I did not forget," said Peggy pointedly. "I said so, but Mr. Mock had already hung up."

A young man ran up in great excitement and shouted cheerfully: "Hello, giant kids! Hello, Peggy!" He almost acted as though he were a school friend of theirs.

"Hello," Peggy replied amiably.

"I'm from the press," the young man shouted, and waved a newspaper over his head. He had beautiful teeth and looked very nice.

"We were all in Mildendo and waited for you there—that's why we're late. We thought you were going to march on our capital, do you see? Well, when we learned that suddenly you had turned up in Plips, we beat it, I can tell you! We covered the three miles in less than half an hour. After all, you're the biggest sensation since Gulliver, and in those days newspapers didn't exist. My name is Richard

Gribles, but just call me Dick. I'm from the *Mildendo News*. Have you seen your picture in the noon edition already?"

"Our picture?" Peggy asked excitedly, and grabbed the paper. "Where?"

"Right on the front page! Big feature!"

"Oh, here it is," called Peggy.

The paper was much larger than the extra edition of the *Plips Morning Post*. It was almost the size of a playing card, and the whole front page was taken up by one photograph. Only at the bottom was there any print: "First authentic photograph of the terrible giants." It showed the children standing on the expressway near the tollbooths. Peggy and Ralph were staring at the sky, waving their green twigs. Peggy was shouting something, her mouth open so wide that you could see way down her throat.

"No, no, no! I look like a witch!" Peggy was horrified. But even so she was very proud of her picture in the newspaper. Probably all of Lilliput was looking at it right now. At home nobody would ever think of putting her picture into the paper.

"Am I in it, too?" asked Jim, and slid over to her on his knees.

"Unfortunately you are," growled Ralph. The

photograph showed Jim just when he was aiming at the helicopter with his gun.

"My gun—!" called Jim. "Can I have my gun back now?"

"No, you won't get it back until we're on our way home," Ralph said with a grunt.

"The telegram," cried Peggy in consternation. "We'd almost forgotten it. Mr. Sergeant! Mr. Sergeant!"

"At your service," called the sergeant, elbowing his way through to them.

"You were going to send the telegram for us."

"Oh, yes, ah . . . well . . ." murmured the sergeant, and pulled the blank out of his pocket.

"A telegram?" Lieutenant Boll exclaimed in surprise.

The mayor, too, was taken aback. "What kind of a telegram?" he asked.

"The children are anxious to send a wire home," reported the sergeant reluctantly. He gave the blank to the mayor.

The mayor took it and read it. Then he looked at the sergeant and shook his head. "But, Sergeant! This would violate the constitution. Just imagine if we had a lot of giants visiting us all of a sudden; it would ruin the entire island!"

"I thought as much," murmured the sergeant unhappily.

"Unfortunately, we cannot send this telegram," the mayor said regretfully. With that he tore up the blank and put the pieces in his pocket.

The children looked at him, aghast.

18

Sheer Paradise

Around them all was silent. There was some heat lightning on the horizon, and a moment later a faint grumble rolled in from the distance. But no one paid any attention to it. The crowd just stared at the children and even the movie cameras ceased their grinding.

"But if we can't send a wire, nobody will be able to come for us," Ralph said, completely unnerved.

"And how will we ever get home then?" Peggy cried out in despair.

"There's always the rubber raft," suggested Jim meekly.

"No, no," Peggy replied quickly. "I'll never set foot in it again!"

"We wouldn't permit that anyway," said the mayor firmly. "It's much too dangerous."

Peggy pushed back her hair. "But, please, please,

Mr. Mayor," she implored him. "We don't want to be giants for the rest of our lives. And our poor parents. That way, we'll never see them again!"

"School starts next month." Ralph looked most concerned.

"School . . . !" Peggy exclaimed. "And I was supposed to get a new dress for school opening!"

"But my dear giant child," the mayor interrupted her, "who said that you were to stay in Lilliput? We wouldn't want that ourselves, as much as we like you. You will go home in a seaworthy motor yacht comfortably, quickly, and easily."

"What?" Peggy cried, flabbergasted. "In a motor yacht?"

"Boy," cried Jim, "and I'll be at the helm."

"Not on your life," Ralph growled angrily, but he too was delighted about the yacht.

"I'm so happy," Peggy stammered and began to cry. The sudden turn for the good was more than she could bear. Nervously, she fumbled for a handkerchief inside her bag without finding it. "Oh, dear," she whimpered. "I've even lost my hanky." She needed to blow her nose.

"Fraser!" the mayor commanded a young man. "Quickly, drive to the Mintz department store and buy the finest and largest bed sheet! Don't bother to have it wrapped. Haste is of the essence!"

"Very well, Your Lordship! They happen to be having a White Sale, and I'll get it at a much reduced price," said Mr. Fraser, and hurried over to his car.

"Never mind the cost," the mayor called after him. "Have them send the bill to the government!"

"Very well, Your Lordship," replied Mr. Fraser with enthusiasm, and drove off. Ralph, in the meantime, had become skeptical. "Will we fit into the boat?" he asked incredulously.

"Three times over," the mayor said reassuringly. "It isn't a Lilliputian boat but one from the world of giants. It was blown onto our shore in a storm. The yacht has a powerful motor, a compass, and an emergency sail. She's in perfect condition."

"Hurrah!" shouted Jim. "Can we go right away?"

"Well, not that quickly," smiled the mayor. "First we have to fill the tank with gasoline and grease the motor. That will take all night. You won't be able to put out to sea until tomorrow morning. Besides, we'll only let you go if the weather is fair. The yacht is lying in an inland port. Twelve tugboats will tow you down the river to Allenbeck on the west coast."

"Will we have to sit on the grass until tomorrow morning?" Peggy asked anxiously. She thought with disgust of her night on the beach.

"But, dear Peggy, we wouldn't let you spend the night in the open! It looks threateningly like a thunderstorm. I very much fear it will rain. The yacht has a cabin. Twenty-seven men of the Sanitation Department are at this moment cleaning it up. As soon as they've finished, you can move in." He looked at his tiny wristwatch. "I'd say that would be in half an hour, perhaps even sooner. You can have your meals in the cabin. That makes sense. The Grand Hotel has most kindly offered to look after you. They'll send over the food in their largest cauldrons. Mr. Mock!" he called. "Have you already spoken to the chef?"

"Everything has been arranged, Your Lordship. I've just been to the hotel," Mr. Mock reported, full of zeal. "We've figured out that each of the giant children will require fifty portions of each course. The head waiter gave me tonight's menu to take along." He pulled a tiny card out of his pocket and began to read: "As appetizer there is paté of goose liver on toast. Then green turtle soup. After that poached filet of sole with mushrooms. The main course is grilled rack of lamb, young parsley potatoes, and asparagus tips. For dessert they will serve ice cream parfait with wafers, strawberry tarts, fruit, cheese, and candied nuts. Of course, we can't offer wine to the children but they can have fruit juice or orangeade. For breakfast they'll get coffee, milk, or chocolate."

"Chocolate!" shouted Jim.

"That's sheer paradise," exclaimed Peggy.

Ralph was speechless. Even at the Warners's, who were very well off, he never had eaten such delicacies.

"Here, here's the bed sheet," panted Mr. Fraser as he ran up with a neatly folded white sheet under his arm. He stood tiptoe and placed it on Peggy's lap.

"Oh, thanks a lot," Peggy said gratefully, and unfolded it. It was as small and dainty as one of Aunt Cornelia's handkerchiefs. She dabbed her eyes with it and blew her nose gently. Then she wanted to return it.

"But no, you must keep it," said the mayor. "You can't travel without a handkerchief."

"Thanks with all my heart." Peggy was touched by his kindness and put the sheet in her shoulder bag.

"Excuse me," said Ralph, "but is the boat far from here?"

He knew that Peggy and Jim were very tired. He was not eager to walk a long distance either.

"For you, the boat is not very far," said the mayor. "We'll take you there later. It lies at the foot of the Station Boulevard, right at the River Parkway, which is opposite the Tippoli Amusement Park and

the zoo. The boat, in a way, is part of the sights there. The town is happy to make you a present of it because you behaved so well and didn't break anything in Lilliput."

Peggy and Ralph thanked him politely.

"An amusement park?" asked Jim eagerly. He had never been in an amusement park. It was always Peggy who was allowed to go to Sydney. Apparently Aunt Cornelia had no desire to invite Jim too.

"Are there roller coasters, merry-go-rounds, and clowns?"

"No clowns," said the mayor with a grin. "But there are merry-go-rounds and many other attractions. There's also a roller-skating rink and above all the giant Ferris wheel."

"A giant wheel?" Jim's eyes popped wide open. "What's that?"

"Can't you see the wheel, with the big cabs dangling from it, over there above the rooftops?"

"Yes," gasped Jim in great excitement.

"That's the giant Ferris wheel. It turns slowly, and when you've reached the top, you can look over all of Plips and its surroundings. Queen Alice donated it as she is very fond of children. She has a daughter of her own, Princess Elsie. The princess is six years old and uses it each year at least ten times."

"That must be nifty," Jim called, and jumped up. He stepped over the mayor, the sergeant, Lieutenant Boll, and Mr. Mock and ran down the street.

"Jim, Jim," Peggy yelled in horror.

"Jim, come back immediately!" shouted Ralph.

"I'll just take a look at the amusement park. I'll be right back," called Jim, and raced down the Station Boulevard toward the river. Suddenly, running did not seem to bother him in the least.

On the sidewalks, lining each side of the street, the Lilliputians stood petrified.

19

Lilliputians Are Not Toys

It was beginning to get dark and lights had been turned on in many houses. Even the streetlights went on suddenly. Again, there was heat lightning on the horizon, but now it was much brighter and followed quickly by the grumbling of thunder.

"Sergeant Thompson!" the mayor called sternly. "Bring the boy back at once."

The sergeant jumped into his car and chased after Jim with his siren shrieking.

But Jim was much too fast for the tiny car, and he disappeared around a corner, behind a row of buildings. All one could see was his shock of hair streaming by behind the chimney tops.

Helplessly, Peggy and Ralph sat on the lawn. Once they had recovered from their initial shock, the Lilliputians poured into the street to get a better view of the sergeant and Jim. This made it impossible for Peggy and Ralph to run after him.

"Oh dear, oh dear," Peggy whispered to Ralph. "I hope that he won't do anything foolish."

Ralph remained silent and bit his lips.

Suddenly, the excited crackle of the loudspeaker sounded from the roof of Lieutenant Boll's car. "Lieutenant, Lieutenant, here's Sergeant Thompson."

The lieutenant grabbed the microphone: "Sergeant, Sergeant, did you catch him?" he asked.

"Almost," squawked the sergeant.

"Almost? Well, where is he?"

"I can see him. He's in the amusement park and is turning the giant Ferris wheel. There are people sitting in the cabs. They were looking down from there on Gulliver Square to get a good view of the giants. They're shouting to make him stop. But he isn't paying any attention to them. Yes he is! He's running off. Now he's approaching the roller coaster. Wait! The superintendent is coming. He's scolding him. Great Gulliver! The boy has lifted him on top of the roller coaster."

"Go ahead and arrest him!" the lieutenant yelled.

"I can't," squawked the sergeant.

"Why?"

"I'm sitting on the roof of the roller-skating palace."

Peggy and Ralph turned pale. They suspected

the worst. Around them there was a hushed silence. Everyone was listening tensely, with bated breath, to the conversation between the lieutenant and the sergeant.

"On the roof of the roller-skating palace?" asked the lieutenant, completely rattled. "How in Mully-Ully-Gue did you ever get up there?"

"I caught up with him in the park, Lieutenant, and ordered him to come with me at once. 'Right away,' he said. 'Just let me take a look around,' and with that he was going to run off again. So, I stepped on the gas and bumped his big toe to make him obey. That made him mad and he put me on the roof."

"Oh, oh," the Lilliputians cried in horror.

"But, Sergeant, how is it that you can talk with me? Where is your microphone?" the lieutenant asked in complete amazement.

"He set me on the roof, car and all," yelled the sergeant, his voice cracking. He seemed to be close to a breakdown.

"Unbelievable!" called the mayor, beside himself with indignation. "How dare he! We Lilliputians are not toys! Lieutenant, send in an alarm to the firehouse. Have them send the hook and ladder company so that they can get the sergeant down from the roof. Issue arms to your men. We have no patience with naughty children here."

"Brax! Miller! Holst! Get your arms," ordered Lieutenant Boll. "Get your automatics from the barracks."

"Ralph, Ralph," gasped Peggy, looking deathly pale. "They're going to shoot him!"

Ralph just groaned and stared helplessly at the policemen.

Brax, Miller, and Holst were running to their cars when there was a blinding flash and a deafening thunderclap, and then a torrent of rain descended on Plips.

"It's raining! It's raining! Everyone run for safety!" the Lilliputians shouted in a state of panic as they crowded into the nearest houses. His cape flowing behind him, the mayor fled into the town hall, followed by the other ladies and gentlemen. The police sought cover by squeezing into their cars. Only the little horses, their heads drooping, were left on the pavement.

Suddenly, Gulliver Square was completely abandoned. Puddles formed at once and no automobile, motorcycle, or even the fire trucks, could have moved without sinking in the puddles. The canals were of little use; there was too much water for them to drain quickly.

"Let's go!" called Ralph. "We've got to catch up with Jim before it's too late." He raced through the puddles, across the square, toward the Station Boulevard.

"Ralph! Ralph! Wait for me!" Peggy yelled, running after him. "I can't keep up with you."

"You've got to," said Ralph. "Every second counts." He waited impatiently until she had caught up with him and both ran around the corner where Jim had disappeared behind the houses.

Now they were running through a narrow, crooked street, rubbing their shoulders against the houses. Ralph's sleeve got caught on a balcony with flowerpots. The balcony tore off and fell on Peggy's foot.

"Ouch! Ouch!" Peggy yelled and hopped on one leg in pain.

"What's the matter?" called Ralph, and turned around anxiously.

"A balcony fell on my foot! Can't you be more careful?"

Ralph was mortified. He had not noticed that he had torn off the balcony.

"Great Scott!" he exclaimed. "Now I've broken something! That's all Jim's fault. How I'd like to get my hands on him!"

Peggy kneeled down, trying to gather up the flowers, but Ralph cried: "Let it go! We have no time for that! We'll have to escape with Jim. As long as it rains, they can't follow us."

He ran on and Peggy tried to keep up with him. "Escape?" she cried. "Where to?"

"To the rubber raft," called Ralph.

"Help! Never!" Peggy croaked. "Can't we escape on the motor yacht?"

"No, there's no gas in it," called Ralph.

"But I don't want to go home in the rubber raft," Peggy cried, and refused to budge.

Ralph came back and pushed her along. "Maybe you want them to shoot Jim?" he lashed out at her.

Horrified, Peggy did not answer.

They had reached the end of the boulevard and could see the giant Ferris wheel ahead of them. Towering above the trees, it stood in the center of a large park dotted with merry-go-rounds, roller coasters, shooting galleries, and pavilions.

"Where's Jim?" Peggy called nervously.

In the fading light they could see him nowhere.

"First we have to rescue the sergeant," said Ralph, and ran up to a big building made entirely of glass and aluminum. He had discovered the police car. It was lying on the domed roof, leaning against a railing.

One door was open. The sergeant had disappeared. Peggy covered her face with both hands. "Jim has kidnapped the sergeant," she cried.

"Nonsense!" growled Ralph. He looked into the

building through a round window. "I can see him."

The sergeant must have escaped through the skylight. High above the skating rink, he was just sliding down a thin steel girder toward a platform from which steps led to the ground. Fortunately, his back was turned toward Peggy and Ralph. They held their breath until he had reached safety. Then they ran on in search of Jim. The lightning and thunder had slackened, but the rain was still coming down in torrents. It pounded on the tin roof of the skating rink like machine-gun fire.

By now, Peggy was soaked to the skin and her hair was dripping.

She had left her cap on the lawn. In the excitement, Ralph had left his tropical helmet behind, too.

"Where can Jim be?" asked Peggy.

The giant Ferris wheel stood motionless. In one of the cabs, a number of Lilliputians were crouching low to hide from the children.

Gingerly, Ralph turned the wheel until the cab with its passengers had reached the ground so that they could leave it after the rain had stopped. Then he took Peggy by the hand and ran toward the roller coaster. There they spied Jim.

20

Monkey Business

On the far side of the park stood an iron structure about ten feet high, resembling a miniature Eiffel Tower. Six gondolas hung on wires attached to the top. They were about the size of the vacuum sweeper in the children's home and were whirling around in a circle so fast that they were flung high above the ground. Jim sat astride one of the gondolas. His shirt tails were fluttering, his face was whipped by the rain, and he was holding tightly onto the wires.

Peggy and Ralph ran up to him.

"Get down from there at once!" yelled Ralph, panting and furious.

"I can't!" howled Jim, and shot past them like a cannonball. When he came around again, he yelled: "I can't reach the switch anymore!" And with that, he was gone.

"Where is the switch?" called Ralph.

"Below the tower," Jim cried. "Help! I'm getting dizzy." And then he disappeared again.

Ralph crawled over to the switch and pulled the lever until the gondolas slowed down. At last, they came to a standstill.

Jim jumped off and tumbled right into a puddle. "Oh, boy, that was great!" he murmured as though he were drunk. Ralph took him by the shoulders and shook him hard.

"Jumping kangaroo! Have you gone completely crazy?"

"I couldn't reach the switches anymore," stuttered Jim. "The thing started to fly high through the air."

"The Lilliputians want to shoot you," cried Peggy excitedly.

Jim jumped up and looked about fearfully. "Why? I've done no harm!"

"You fooled with the people on the Ferris wheel and you put the sergeant on the roof," Ralph growled. "Now we have to flee on account of you."

"We'll have to escape in the rubber raft and we won't get anything more to eat. All those good things," Peggy hissed angrily.

"I just wanted to put the sergeant out of my way," Jim stammered.

"Shut your big mouth," growled Ralph. "Let's

go! Quick! We've got to get to the beach before the rain stops."

Jim was dazed. He still could not understand why they had to leave so suddenly. Again he looked around nervously to make sure that nobody was taking aim at him.

"How will we ever get to the beach?" Peggy whimpered. "We can't use the train when it's dark."

"We'll wade the river," said Ralph. He had already thought out a plan of escape. "The Mayor said the river flows into the ocean near Allenbeck on the west coast. That's very near where we landed. Besides, they won't look for us in the river. They're sure to think that we'll take the expressway back. Let's go now," he urged. "The rain is beginning to let up."

"But I can't run," growled Jim. "My big toe hurts so."

"Serves you right," Ralph said grimly, and started off. Peggy raced behind him. Jim followed.

"Ralph, do you really know where the river is?" panted Peggy.

"Somewhere back there. I saw the railway bridge a little while ago."

They hurdled a small stone wall and found themselves once more in a park. A narrow, winding path led them past a number of houses and cottages that looked like stables. They stood on patches of lawn or sand fenced off by wire enclosures. As they raced by, the children could hear eerie noises that sounded like neighing, hissing, growling, and grunting.

"What are those horrid sounds?" whispered Peggy.

"There must be some kind of animals here," said Ralph with a frown. "Be careful that you don't step on them."

It had now grown completely dark, and they could barely make out the gravel path. Here and there, tiny electric lamps lit the way. Once in a while the sky flashed with the fleeting lightning of the receding storm.

"Look out!" cried Ralph. "There's a sharp turn in the path here." He turned to the left in the nick of time. Peggy bumped her foot against a low fence and tumbled over a ditch into a sandpile.

Jim shot past her, in pursuit of Ralph.

"Help! Help! I'm covered with monkeys!" Peggy howled at the top of her voice.

Aghast, Ralph and Jim stopped in their tracks.

"What's the matter?" cried Ralph.

"I'm covered with monkeys!" Peggy howled again.

"What kind of monkeys?" asked Ralph, completely rattled.

"I've no idea!" screamed Peggy. "Come and help me."

Ralph and Jim ran back. Peggy sat beside the ditch in a sand hole between several landscaped rocks. Miniature apes were crawling all over her. They were chattering angrily because Peggy had stirred them up.

"Great boomerang!" cried Ralph. "We've walked into a zoo!"

"My hair!" protested Peggy. Five or six tiny monkeys sat on her head, tangling her hair.

"Jump into the moat and put your head under the water," called Jim. "Then they'll swim away."

Without a moment's hesitation, Peggy jumped into the water and dove under. The little monkeys quickly swam back to their rock island. They could not climb over the fence because the wall of the moat was too steep.

Peggy kept her head under water until she almost suffocated. At last, she came up for air, coughing and choking, her arms reaching out for Ralph and Jim. Quickly, Ralph and Jim pulled her out because the little monkeys were crouching, ready to jump at her again.

"Eeeks!" Peggy complained, out of breath. "Those monkeys were disgusting! They pinched me!"

"But I told you to watch out," Ralph said irritably. "We've walked into the zoo."

"How should I know?" Peggy protested angrily.

"Who would think of monkeys?" She wrung out her hair and shook her head to get the water out of her ears.

"Hurry," Ralph urged her impatiently.

"Just a minute," said Peggy. "First, I have to take off my shoes because they're full of water." She sat down on top of a cage. The thin iron bars holding up the roof yielded under her weight and out shot a tiger. He was only the size of a toy cat, but he looked like a real tiger. He switched his tail, opened his mouth, and let out a roar.

"Good heavens!" cried Ralph. "The tiger is loose!"

Frightened, the tiger took one leap and disappeared into the darkness.

"We must catch him," yelled Ralph and ran after him.

Frantically, they looked for him everywhere, but they could not find him.

"He's gone," said Peggy in dismay.

"We've *got* to find him." Ralph groaned. "If we don't, he'll kill everybody."

"There he is! I see him!" Peggy called, excitedly. High up in a tree, two glowing embers were looking down at them. She tiptoed over to the tree slowly. "Here, pussy, here pussy, here pussy," she begged. "Please come down from there."

The tiger just hissed angrily.

Peggy wanted to touch him, but he waved his paw and almost scratched her.

"Hey," she shouted. "What a mean pussy you are!"

"Let me try," called Jim, "I know how to catch tigers. You have to grab them by the neck." Stealthily, he crept up from behind, but the tiger whipped around and bit him on his nose.

"Ouch!" howled Jim, and felt his nose.

"Let me see," said Peggy, horrified.

Jim took his hand away and Peggy looked at his nose anxiously. There was only a little bleeding.

"Don't make such a fuss," she said. "The tiger is only a tiny one, after all."

"But it hurts," Jim insisted with a whimper.

Meanwhile, Ralph stalked the tiger from the other side and succeeded in grabbing him by the neck. He held him as far away from himself as he could because the tiger was squirming violently.

"We must lock him up somewhere quickly," he called and looked about.

"Here," said Peggy, and opened a cage. A lion stuck out his head. "Oh, no!" cried Peggy, and slammed shut the gate. "I almost let a lion out, too!" She groaned.

"Where the dickens can we put the tiger?" called Ralph. "I can't hold him much longer."

"In my bag!" Peggy proposed, and held out her shoulder bag. Ralph dropped the tiger inside and closed it. The tiger seemed to be quite happy. He no longer struggled or growled.

"Now, let's beat it," said Ralph. "We've lost too much time already."

Peggy was beside herself. "How do you expect me to run around with a tiger in my bag?" she cried.

Ralph scratched his head. "Shucks, you're right. What shall we do? You've ruined his cage and all the other cages are full." His eyes fell on Jim's helmet. "I've got it!" he called. "Jim, let me have your helmet."

"Why?" protested Jim. He was determined to hold onto it after having given up his treasured gun, but Ralph pulled the helmet off Jim's head.

"My helmet, my helmet," howled Jim. "Give me my helmet!"

"I'll give you something right on your nose," Ralph retorted angrily. "As though we didn't have you to blame for all this!"

Ruefully, Jim kept quiet. Ralph took the tiger by the neck and pulled him out of the bag. He put him down on the gravel walk and quickly covered him up with the helmet. Then he banked gravel around the brim and packed it down to make sure that the tiger would not escape.

"Will he have air to breathe?" asked Peggy, concerned.

"Plenty," said Ralph. "There are enough vent holes in the helmet. Let me have your pencil."

Peggy handed him her pencil, and Ralph scribbled all over the white helmet: "Caution! Tiger!!" with lots of exclamation marks. Still not satisfied, he drew a number of arrows pointing down at the brim. By this time it had grown completely dark. Warily, they proceeded in single file in order not to trip over any other fences or wire enclosures.

Again, they bumped into a small wall, but after stepping over it they at last stood on the parkway at the shore of the river. They listened anxiously, but all they could hear was the gurgle of the river. The rain was now only a drizzle. The light of a few isolated streetlamps was reflected in the puddles that had formed on the pavement.

Peggy and Jim were so exhausted that they sat down on the riverbank and dangled their legs in the water. They could not see the opposite shore.

"Wait here; I want to see how deep the river is," said Ralph in a hushed voice. He waded in and disappeared into the darkness. He returned, looking very dejected.

"The water reaches up to my chest. I'm afraid that both of you will have to swim."

"I won't swim in a strange river. There might be crocodiles in it," Peggy cried with a shudder.

"If there really are, they would only be the size of lizards," suggested Ralph.

"The monkeys were very small, too, but even so they pinched hard," Peggy complained.

"I won't swim in the dark," mumbled Jim. "My nose hurts and my toe and heel are sore. I want to go home."

"If you act like that, we'll never get home," Ralph exclaimed impatiently. "I wish we had a float or something like it. I could pull you behind me."

"Perhaps we will find the motor cruiser," said Peggy. "Didn't the mayor say that it was docked here near the parkway?"

"Nonsense," growled Ralph. "It would be much too big for me to pull."

"We could drift in it," said Jim.

"Oh, dear," called Peggy, "what about the men from the Sanitation Department who are cleaning up the cabin?"

"Stay here," Ralph said sternly. "Perhaps I can find something to use as a boat." He disappeared again and presently they could hear him call cheerfully, "Come here, come here! I found a barge. You two will just fit into it." Peggy and Jim ran up to him. On the river shore lay an empty barge about the size of the small flat-bottomed boat in which they paddled around the duck pond at home. Quickly, Peggy and Jim got in. They could even stretch out in it. Ralph loosened his belt and also took Jim's. He joined the two belts together and fastened one end to the barge. Then he waded into the river and pulled Peggy and Jim behind him. Most of the time he walked on the bottom, but once in a while he had to swim and take the belt between his teeth. The current helped him along, and soon he could hear the murmur of the ocean. At his right he could see the pale glimmer of the beach. He pushed the barge through the heavy bulrushes and after he reached the shore made it fast to a pole with the belts so that it would not drift out with the tide. It had stopped raining and he looked around nervously. The low forest, with its funny little trees, strung along the coast like a black snake. A faint roar sounded in the distance. It sounded like a helicopter.

"Peggy! Jim!" Ralph called tensely. "We've arrived. Hurry, hurry, you've got to get out!"

Peggy and Jim had fallen asleep, and he had to

shake them to wake them. Peggy sat bolt upright. "Where am I?" she stammered.

"We're on the beach, and we've got to hurry. It has stopped raining and it isn't quite as dark anymore."

Peggy scrambled onto the shore, stretched herself, and yawned. Jim jumped out with one big leap and then collapsed with a groan. "My toe, my toe!" he howled. He pulled off his sneaker and stared at his foot. His toe had swollen to the size of a big boil. Then he gingerly felt his nose. It, too, was swollen. Helpless, he stared at Ralph and Peggy. They had to support him on either side while he hopped along on one leg, moaning and groaning. Peggy stumbled frequently, and even Ralph had to use his last ounce of strength to hold himself up. Their clothes were wet and dirty. Peggy had left her cap behind, and Ralph and Jim were without their helmets and belts. Jim had only one shoe left. Peggy's hair was a hopeless wet tangle.

"I can't continue," complained Peggy from time to time.

But Ralph kept urging her on. "Don't quit. We haven't much further to go. We're almost there."

When they reached the path that they had discovered early in the morning, Ralph exclaimed cheerfully: "Now it's only fifty paces more. I counted them this morning so that we could find our raft again." He counted out loud, and when he got to fifty, he stopped and looked around. "Great boomerang!" he murmured hoarsely.

The rubber raft had disappeared.

21

The Shore Was Blown Away

Dawn was breaking. Thick, black clouds lay on the horizon, and far out, above the sea, there was an occasional flash of lightning.

On the edge of the forest, where their raft had been, the children sat in silence and stared glumly at the sand. The wind whispered mournfully in the leaves of the small trees, and the surf pounded like muted kettledrums.

Suddenly, the sirens started up again. Instinctively, Jim crouched low.

"They're after us," breathed Peggy.

"They won't find us as long as it's dark," Ralph said tonelessly.

"But it will be daylight soon . . ." Peggy stopped and held her breath.

From somewhere in the forest came a soft and continuous hum.

"Those are the helicopters," she cried, and clutched Ralph's arm.

"Those aren't helicopters, that's a car," said Ralph shakily. The hum came closer and closer, and then the narrow beam of a searchlight hit the water and scanned the waves. Then it swung around and pinpointed the children.

"Hit the ground!" Ralph hissed.

They threw themselves flat and pressed against the damp, cool sand as if to seek protection.

The noise of the motor came closer, and a familiar voice called: "Well, here you are," and Mr. Krumps appeared on his tractor right in front of their feet.

Astonished, the children sat up.

"Mr. Krumps!" Peggy cried.

Mr. Krumps shut off the motor and gave them a friendly nod. He drew big puffs of smoke from his pipe, and his white hair flowed in the cool wind. A muffler was tied around his neck.

"By jove! You look a bit the worse for wear! I learned from the radio that you had run away. Reckon you want to get home quickly. Right?"

"Oh, yes," Peggy moaned in despair. "But we can't because our rubber raft has disappeared."

"Just take it easy," said Mr. Krumps. "Here it is." He pointed with his pipe behind his shoulder.

Tied to the rear of the tractor lay the raft with the paddles and even Jim's gun. Ralph and Peggy were speechless.

"Great boomerang!" Ralph gulped at last.

"My gun!" Overjoyed, Jim jumped up only to fall back with a groan. He had forgotten about his sore toe.

"Where did you find our raft?" Ralph asked.

"I kind of figured you would need it again. I hid it back in the woods, between the thatch and the river. The tide is liable to run way up on the beach and sweep everything out to sea. Now, come clean. What sort of mischief have you been up to?" He looked at them sternly. "I hope that you didn't hurt or kill anyone. If you did, I'll have to call the police."

"Upon our word of honor, we haven't hurt or killed anyone," Peggy assured him quickly.

"Hm, can't say that I heard any mention of it on the radio . . . as far as I could make anything of all that chatter." He gave Jim a penetrating stare and pointed his pipe at him. "That boy there put the sergeant on the roof and the Superintendent of Parks on the roller coaster. He played with the giant Ferris wheel when people were sitting in it."

Jim turned pale. "I just wanted . . . I didn't . . ."

he stammered meekly. "And I'll never do it again," he promised, conscious of his guilt.

"Rot!" Mr. Krumps interrupted him disapprovingly. "Just because you're so big you thought you could do what you wanted. Right? Size is no virtue, my lad, remember that." He took his pipe out of his mouth and spat with an air of disdain. "Nobody likes to be pushed around. Do you understand? Not so sure whether you shouldn't be left to sweat this out alone. But I feel sorry for your sister and her friend."

"Ralph accidentally tore off a balcony," Peggy confessed. "And I busted the tiger's cage," she added meekly.

"Is that so?" growled Mr. Krumps. "Giants have no business in Lilliput. Reckon you're best off at home. But do you really want to go in that thing there?" He pointed to the rubber raft. "I wouldn't put out to sea in it, not for a million onzes. You had better stay here and take what's coming to you. Perhaps they'll just lock you up."

"But I don't want to be locked up!" exclaimed Peggy in horror. "I've never been locked up in my life!"

"Well, it's no picnic. 'Way back, they locked me up for three days because I exploded those firecrackers. That's strictly forbidden. I deserved it.

Let the punishment fit the crime. I wouldn't do that sort of thing any more. Now, think it over carefully. Once you've left the mirage behind you, you can never return."

"Mirage?" Ralph asked earnestly.

Since they had drifted in during the night, they had not been aware of a mirage.

"My soul, don't you know what a mirage is?"

"Oh, I know what it is," said Peggy happily. "A mirage is a fata morgana."

"Fata morgana? Don't know anything about that," said Mr. Krumps briskly.

"A fata morgana is when in the desert you see an oasis that does not exist," Peggy explained proudly. "Our teacher, Miss Lampart, told us about it. She knows a lot. And Aunt Cornelia once was in the desert herself and saw something that didn't exist."

"All right, all right!" Mr. Krumps interrupted her impatiently. "Here it's the other way around. Lilliput is surrounded by a layer of air that makes it vanish. That's the reason people don't find us so easily, thank heavens! By jove! I almost forgot. Did Pastor Krog give you anything to eat?"

"Pastor Krog is in Tottenham on the west coast," said Peggy. "But the police fed us and it tasted awfully good."

"My soul! What's Pastor Krog up to in Totten-

207

ham? You couldn't drag me there with a team of horses. Well, I guess people just travel everywhere these days. But I'm glad that at least you got something to eat. I couldn't have brought you anything. My wife and my mother-in-law were still asleep. I know better than to wake them up so early." He grinned but suddenly became serious again.

"I must warn you again. Once you have left the curtain of air behind you, it's too late. I'd hate to see anything happen to you."

Ralph got up. "Many thanks," he said, and looked around to be sure nobody was in sight. "We're lucky. The wind is out of the west and will push us toward home. The ocean is fairly calm, and the overcast sky will help protect us from sunburn."

"Well, then, be off with you," said Mr. Krumps. "It's beginning to get light. Reckon the sun will rise pretty soon."

Now Peggy got up. "We don't know how to thank you for everything, Mr. Krumps," she said warmly.

"Nonsense," said Mr. Krumps, and sucked hard on his pipe. "I was young once myself. Good luck." He started the motor and switched on his headlights.

Quickly, Ralph untied the raft from the tractor. Then he pulled it down to the beach and shoved it into the water. As luck would have it, the wind blew from the shore and the breakers were very gentle. "Let's go!" he called to Peggy and Jim impatiently, as he squinted at the clouds above. The early rays of the rising sun gave them a rosy hue. Peggy ran down the beach and jumped into the raft. Jim followed on his hands and knees. He was too tired even to hop on one leg, and Ralph lifted him into the raft. He pushed it out into deeper water until it was afloat and then he jumped in and began to paddle. Once again he sat in the stern.

"Jim, you have to paddle too," he called.

"I can't, my nose hurts too much." Jim groaned. He was lying in the bottom, hugging his gun.

"Let me paddle," Peggy volunteered. She crouched on her knees and began to paddle eagerly. There were only ripples on the water and the raft was quite steady. Ralph and Peggy turned around to wave to Mr. Krumps. Mr. Krumps was just turning into the narrow path with the white line in the center. He tooted his horn a few times as a farewell salute. Then he disappeared.

Doggedly, Peggy and Ralph resumed paddling. The shoreline receded quickly until the forest with the odd, small trees was only a dark line. Suddenly, there was a roar above them, and a helicopter appeared from out of the clouds. It had blue and white stripes with a golden crown in a red field.

"Help!" cried Peggy and crouched low on the raft. "Now they're going to drop bombs on us."

Ralph was paralyzed with fear. The helicopter came lower and lower and hovered directly above their heads. A side door opened, and Sergeant Thompson leaned out. Behind him stood Lieutenant Boll, holding onto him.

"Children, children," shouted the sergeant through a megaphone. "For Gulliver's sake, come back at once! Queen Alice has pardoned you. You will be allowed to go home in the motor cruiser."

Peggy sat up and gazed at him with her mouth wide open.

"Quick, quick, turn around!" the sergeant shouted again. "We have taken the motor cruiser down to the estuary."

"Hurray!" Peggy cried jubilantly.

Ralph turned the raft around and paddled with all his might. Peggy, too, paddled like mad, but the wind was freshening and pushed them out to sea.

In despair, Ralph cried: "We can't paddle against the wind!"

The helicopter was still hovering above them, and the sergeant threw out a thin cable. Ralph caught it and tied it to the rope that was looped around the raft. Slowly, the helicopter gained height in an attempt to pull the raft behind it. Then suddenly the cable broke and the helicopter vanished. The shore-line, too, seemed to have been blown away.

"We've penetrated the layer of air," Ralph murmured hoarsely.

"Oh, oh!" cried Peggy. Once more she threw herself down, buried her head in her arms, and wept.

Ralph set his jaw firmly and continued to paddle toward the open sea. Before long, the sun broke through the clouds and shone down mercilessly from a clear blue sky.

Peggy sat up and looked at Ralph. "I'm terribly hot," she whimpered, "and my sunburn is beginning to hurt again."

Ralph took off his shirt and handed it to her. "Here, cover yourself with it," he ordered.

"But what about you?" protested Peggy.

"I don't need it," growled Ralph. "I don't get sunburned." But he knew that unless they reached home quickly, he would not be spared.

"Thanks," murmured Peggy, and crawled under the shirt.

From time to time, Ralph splashed himself with water. Suddenly he felt dizzy. He slid from the rim of the raft, unconscious.

22

A Tiger Bit Him on the Nose

Peggy woke up. Her eyes smarted and she had to squint. Her body was burning all over, and her head was buzzing like a swarm of bees. Somebody was rocking her gently, and she could hear the steady throb of an engine. Now and then a horn sounded. She sat up and looked around in confusion. She was sitting in a real bed and wearing pajamas that were much too big for her. On the ceiling a fan was turning and on the wall there were three round holes. Beside her bed, on a night table, stood small bottles and a glass with a spoon in it. Next to them lay her shoulder bag. Then she discovered Ralph and Jim. They were lying in two other beds against the opposite wall. Ralph was on his back. He had a white towel over his forehead and was covered up to his chin. She could only see Jim's mop of hair. He did not move.

"Ralph! Ralph! Ralph!" Peggy called in amazement. "Everything is so gigantic. The beds, the chairs, the door! Where are we?"

"On a steamer," murmured Ralph. "Nothing is gigantic. What makes you think so? My head is buzzing."

"Mine is too," said Peggy, "and my tongue is swollen. I can hardly move it."

"We almost died of thirst. My skin is completely afire."

"Why isn't Jim moving?" she asked anxiously.

"I think he's sleeping."

"Ralph, are we going home?" asked Peggy.

"I hope so," Ralph murmured faintly.

"But everything *is* so gigantic," said Peggy. She stopped abruptly when the door opened and two men and a nurse entered. One of the men wore the white coat of a doctor and the other the gold-braided uniform of a captain. The doctor walked up to Peggy and felt her pulse. "Well, how's our little patient doing?" he asked.

"Oh, thank you," said Peggy. "I'm just a little dizzy."

Then the doctor walked over to Ralph and felt his pulse. He didn't disturb Jim.

"Are we very sick?" asked Peggy nervously.

"Sunstroke," replied the doctor calmly. "The big boy has a bad burn. But the little fellow has got it worse. Shock and exhaustion."

Jim sat up and squinted as though he were grinning. That was all one could see of him. His whole head was wrapped in a bandage. He squinted once more, then fell back and dozed off again.

The doctor smiled. "Why, he's already doing a lot better. But from now on he will have to be a bit more careful."

"May I talk to the children for a moment?" the captain asked.

"Of course," said the doctor. "But if you don't mind, keep it short. They need all the rest they can get."

"Hi, Peggy," said the captain, and sat down on the edge of her bed. He had a voice like a foghorn.

"How do you do?" she said politely. "My head is buzzing."

"I can well imagine," said the captain. "After all, you were drifting in your rubber raft for three days and three nights without any food or drink."

"But we had a good breakfast," said Peggy. "I just didn't care for the squid. I drank fifty pails of milk."

"Hmmm," said the captain, and winked at the doctor.

"Pretty high fever," the doctor said smilingly.

"Well, well, milk you say?" said the captain to Peggy. "Now tell me, what do you suppose happened to Jim's nose in the middle of the ocean?"

"A tiger bit him on the nose," said Peggy.

"You don't say? A tiger? Hm! And why didn't you have any covering on your heads? Don't you know how dangerous that is in this terrible heat?"

"Well, it was like this," said Peggy. "We had to run away quickly because we thought they were going to shoot Jim. That's why I had to leave my cap on the lawn and that's why Ralph forgot his tropical helmet. Jim had to part with his because we didn't know what to do with the tiger."

"You don't say," the captain interrupted her quietly. "I suppose we found you in the nick of time."

"But there are no ships around here, are there?" Ralph asked eagerly.

"You had more luck than brains, son," the captain said. "You surely would have been lost if we had not intercepted a mysterious radiogram."

"A radiogram?" Peggy cried excitedly.

"That's right, a radiogram," said the captain, and pulled a long strip of paper out of his pocket. " 'Warner Farm, Long Hill, Near Home, Australia. SOS! SOS! SOS! Peggy, Jim, and Ralph drifting helplessly in raft on ocean Stop Last sighted latitude eighteen degrees nineteen minutes South longitude ninety-eight degrees eighty-five minutes East SOS Save the Children.' " The captain looked up. "Well, with that we raced here at full speed and picked you up. We immediately notified your parents by radio that we had rescued you. They radioed back: 'Overjoyed, all Australia excited about the children.' "

The captain smiled. "You have become real celebrities. Tomorrow we will land in Derby, especially for you. You'll feel better by then. Your parents are coming to fetch you in the car." He rolled up the message and put it back into his pocket. "The big mystery is: Where did the radiogram come from? There is no ship or airplane anywhere near this area!"

"The telegram came from Lilliput," said Peggy, starry-eyed. "I'm sure that Queen Alice ordered it to be sent. She is very fond of children. She has a small daughter, Princess Elsie. The princess loves to ride on the Ferris wheel."

"Oh, you don't say. Why are you so sure that the telegram came from Lilliput?" asked the captain.

"Because we were there," said Peggy proudly.

"Just imagine! You were in Lilliput. That's great! I thought Lilliput only existed in a book."

"We thought so too," said Peggy, "but Mr. Krumps made fun of us."

"I suppose you've read *Gulliver's Travels*, child. Yes?"

Peggy nodded eagerly. "I know it very well. But now Lilliput is completely modern." Although her tongue hurt, she talked on cheerfully. "They don't shoot with bows and arrows any more. They have guns and helicopters and railroads and automobiles. Yes, and skyscrapers. The Lilliputians are charming. Even the police are wonderful. Particularly Sergeant Thompson. If Jim hadn't put him on the roof of the roller-skating rink, we would have come home in a beautiful motor cruiser instead of the stupid rubber raft. We also would have had a delicious dinner. Goose liver paté, turtle soup, filet of sole, rack of lamb, and ice cream parfait. I was looking forward to it so much. Jim spoiled it all. He started to play around with the giant Ferris wheel, which had a lot of people in it, and he put the Superintendent of Parks on top of the roller coaster. I was embarrassed to death. I would have loved to stay on a bit longer." Silently, she began to weep. Her cheeks were hot and her eyes had a feverish glow.

The doctor put his hand on the captain's shoulder.

"There, there, dear child," said the captain

soothingly, and got up. "Don't get excited. It was nothing but a dream."

"Dream?" asked Peggy, shocked.

"Why, of course, child," the captain said with paternal kindness. "What else? Lilliput doesn't exist in reality."

"But Ralph and Jim were there too," Peggy cried excitedly.

"Ralph," called the captain.

"What?" Ralph murmured drowsily.

"Peggy insists that you have been in Lilliput. How about it?"

"Lilliput?" Ralph murmured disdainfully. "I don't know anything about Lilliput."

Peggy was speechless. "There, you see, Peggy," the captain said soothingly. "Didn't I tell you that it was only a dream? Now, lie down and get a good sleep. That way, you will get well quickly, and by the time you get home you will have forgotten all about Lilliput." He stroked her hair and left. Somebody had carefully combed Peggy's hair. It fell to her shoulders smooth and shiny.

"Nurse Rita will give you your medicine later," the doctor said, and nodded at the nurse to leave with him.

Without moving, Peggy sat in her bed lost in

thought. She began to cry and absentmindedly reached for her handkerchief in her shoulder bag. But just as she was about to blow her nose, she stiffened. Then, like lightning, she jumped out of bed and ran over to Ralph, almost falling because she tripped over her long pajama trousers. She kneeled down and shook him.

"Ralph! Ralph!" she called excitedly.

"What now?" asked Ralph suspiciously.

"Here," she said, and held her handkerchief in front of his eyes.

"What do you want me to do with it?" asked Ralph.

"Just read," Peggy ordered him sternly. Attached to the handkerchief was a tiny white tag on which something was printed in even tinier letters.

"I can't read that," murmured Ralph, "my eyes are much too sore."

"Well, then, I'll read it to you," said Peggy. "Department Store Mintz White Sale, Extra Large Bed Sheet, Price 3 onzes, 2 dimelings." She looked at him angrily.

"Hmm," said Ralph with an embarrassed grin.

"Ugh," cried Peggy, "why did you lie?"

Ralph sat up with a jerk. He was wrapped in bandages.

"Jumping kangaroo!" he hissed. "Don't yell so. Don't you understand? If they find Lilliput, they'll ruin it."

For a moment, Peggy looked at him bewildered. Then a happy smile came over her face. "Ralph, you are wonderful," she whispered.

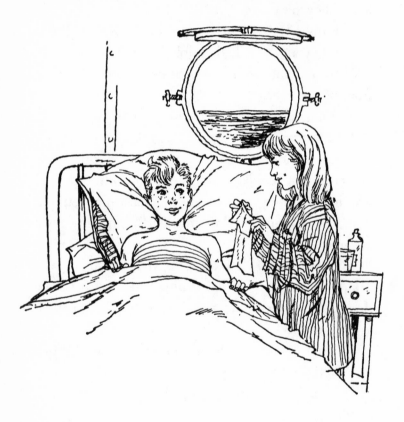

Henry Winterfeld (1901–1990) was born in Germany. He began writing for children in 1933, when he wrote *Trouble at Timpetill* to entertain his son, who was sick with scarlet fever. He went on to write a number of children's books, which have been published around the world.